Rise Of The Darklighter
Book Two:

NIGHT OF THE DEMON

G.W. Mullins

LIGHT OF THE MOON PUBLISHING

ISBN: 978-1-958221-19-8

First Printing

This is a work of fiction. Names, characters, businesses, places, events and incidents are either the products of the author's imagination or used in a fictitious manner. Any resemblance to actual persons, living or dead, or actual events is purely coincidental.

Light Of The Moon Publishing has allowed this work to remain exactly as the author intended, verbatim, without editorial input.

Printed in the United States of America

For further information, on his writing, visit G.W. Mullins' web site at http://gwmullins.wix.com/books

For books available from G.W. Mullins in Hardback, Paperback and eBook

Visit: https://gwmullins.wixsite.com/books

Or scan the QR Code below

Links to G.W. Mullins pages are on Linktree https://linktr.ee/gw.mullins

What begins as a simple, bittersweet tale about a man turned into a polar bear, grandly unfolds into a rich, mythical adventure, in this best-selling book series.

Based on Hans Christian Andersen's fairy tale, author G.W. Mullins expands on this classic story creating a new mythology that takes readers into the land of snow and ice.

G.W. Mullins

Rise Of The Snow Queen
Book Series

The Polar Bear King

War Of The Witches

The Story of Gerda and Kai

Rise Of The Snow Queen Series

What begins as a simple, bittersweet tale about a man turned into a polar bear, grandly unfolds into a rich, mythical adventure in this best-selling book series.

Based on Hans Christian Andersen's fairy tale, author G.W. Mullins expands on this story creating a new mythology that takes readers into the world of snow and ice.

Long before the adventures of Gerda and Kai, this story takes readers to a remote mountain village, where winter claims lives, at the Snow Queen's command. The story goes back to the Mirror and how it cracked, sending its shards into the world to infect the innocent.

This reimagining, embarks on a much more adult tone with the mood turning rather sinister, as the Snow Queen battles to obtain the mirror. The story will capture and pull you in as Gerda and Kai make their appearances by the third book in the series.

Rise Of The Snow Queen Series

Book One: The Polar Bear King

Book Two: The War Of The Witches

Book Three: The Story Of Gerda And Kai

From
The
Dead
Of
Night
Book Series

Death is only the beginning.
Daniel walked in the land of the Dead.
Now the Dead want him back

Daniel Is Waiting

Daniel Returns

Daniel Awakens

Daniel's Fate

G.W.
Mullins

From the Dead Of Night Series

Death Is Only The Beginning. Daniel walked in the land of the dead. Now the dead want him back!

Daniel Stratton died in a tragic accident. His life should have been over, but it was not. His spirit spent the next sixty years trying to communicate with the people who came to the cemetery. Then, Jen came one night to the mausoleum, seeking refuge from a life that was spinning out of control. It was there she found Daniel.

As they work to free him from the cemetery; they learn that the Light comes for all dead, Daniel is forced to enter it. Inside he sees seven Shadow People within the light, and each one marks him. Daniel knows these Shadows will come for him. Each one in the body of human who has just died. To survive, Daniel and Jen must escape the "Shadows" that are coming for them.

From the Dead Of Night Series

Book One: Daniel Is Waiting

Book Two: Daniel Returns

Book Three Daniel Awakens

Book Four: Daniel's Fate

Best-Selling Author G.W. Mullins speaks to the dead and talks about After Death Communication in his book series...
Messages From The Other Side
Stories of the Dead, Their Communication, and Unfinished Business
Messages From The Other Side
G.W. Mullins
Messages From The Other Side
G.W. Mullins
Messages From The Other Side
G.W. Mullins
Crossing Over
Mullins
Crossing Over
Mullins
Crossing Over
Mullins
Messages From The Other Side
Crossing Over
Available in Hardback, Paperback and eBook

Messages From The Other Side Series

Best-selling author G.W. Mullins shares his personal journey towards understanding death, the afterlife and communication with spirits of loved ones who have passed over. In "Messages From The Other Side Stories of the Dead, Their Communication, and Unfinished Business," Mullins tells of dealing with the grief of his mother passing and the reassurance of an after-death communication that totally changed his outlook towards death and grief.

This book not only tells of Mullins' personal journey into understanding but also guides others to understand why we receive communications and the signs to look for. Mullins also explores visitation dreams and tells of his own personal experience in the area and shares the stories of others who have had similar experiences.

This book highlights the author's personal journey in an exploration for knowledge, and his understanding, without question, there is life after death.

Messages From The Other Side Series

Book One: Meassages From The Other Side

Book Two: Crossing Over

In order to save his uncle, Malachi is forced to summon
Santa Muerte, the deity of death. With his soul on the
line, he must do her bidding, to regain his freedom.

To fight evil, you have to
embrace the darkness

Rise
Of The
DarkLighter

From Best-Selling Author

G.W.
Mullins

Dark Awakening
Night Of The Demon
Available in Hardback, Paperback and eBook

Rise Of The Darklighter Series

Mullins returns to the familiar world he created for the "From The Dead Of Night" series, while building a new story in this universe. In the book "Daniel's Fate," Mullins left his audience with an ending that promised more. In this latest book, he delivers with a continuation of the final battle between good and evil.

In order to save his uncle, Malachi is forced to summon Santa Muerte, the deity of death. He offers a year of his life in exchange for her help. With his soul on the line, he must do her bidding, to regain his freedom.

The dead begin to rise, as Angels and Demons prepare to wage war for control of humanity. Malachi must choose a side as Armageddon begins.

"Dark Awakening" is the first of three books from "Rise Of The Darklighter." This new series is a continuation of his "From The Dead Of Night" books.

Rise Of The DarkLighter

Book One: Dark Awakening

Book Two: Night Of The Demon

Danni liked the quiet upstate New York house she had moved to...
Until she realized something else was living in the house with her.

VENGEANCE

G.W. MULLINS

SOMETIMES
THE THINGS YOU CANNOT SEE,
CAN BE THE MOST DEADLY.

G.W.
Mullins

Available worldwide in Hardback, Paperback and eBook

Vengeance
A Paranormal Murder Mystery

*"Mystery, Murder, Paranormal Events, and a story
that leaves you guessing as the bodies stack up."*
– Matthew Trent OutLoud Magazine

After the death of her father, Danni starts a new life
in a seaside town in New York where she and her
mother move into a strange Gothic house with a
terrible history. From the moment Danni gets there,
she feels she is being watched. She is sure they are
not alone in the house.

As Danni learns of her new home, she is told of a
past resident who fell to her death on the nearby cliffs
at the same time that her teenaged daughter,
Elizabeth, disappeared.

Elizabeth's spirit, appears to Danni and claims that
her mother's death was a murder, not suicide and asks
for Danni's help in bringing the dangerous killer to
justice.

The mystery unfolds as Danni enlists the help of the
hunky new friend she has made named Joe. A
romance develops between them, but does Joe know
more about the murder and disappearance than he is
letting on? Will Danni live to solve the murder?

Dream Walker Series

They say a dream is a wish, but what they forgot to mention, nightmares are dreams too. As the city darkens and humans descend into sleep, a powerful being enters the Earth Realm. This mysterious creature, known as the Sandman, takes control of our dreams and battles for control of souls.

After a boy named Zach is taken into the other realm, he awakens to a new world filled with nightmares. He is joined by two others, Daniel and Jen, as they battle to escape the Dream World, and find their way back to reality. Beware the Sandman is coming.

"Enter The Sandman" is the first of three books from Author G.W. Mullins' "Dream Walker" book series. This new series, shares a couple of familiar faces from the Best-Selling "From The Dead Of Night" books, featuring the Best-Selling titles "Daniel Is Waiting" and "Daniel Returns."

Dream Walker Series

Book One: Enter The SandMan

Book Two: Wide Awake In Dreamland

Nick Grainger

Book One

The Curse Of Cleopatra

G.W. Mullins

Nick Grainger Series

Building on the concept that the Earth was once populated by a superior Ancient Alien race, this new book series takes the reader on an adventure through gateways to the multiverse.

Nick Grainger, a young college student working on an archaeological dig in Egypt, accidentally activates a gate to a different universe. He along with three of his companions, are thrown into the ancient alien gateway system between parallel worlds. Lost in the multiverse, they must search for a way home.

On their journey, their gate opens into strange new worlds, similar to their Earth, but in different times and in places. It is on one such Earth, they arrive in Egypt, not as it was in the days of the ancients. Now, it is a place where a technologically advanced race of gods rule.

These new gods of Egypt live through taking the bodies of human hosts. It is there, Nick must fight his ultimate battle, as he is designated to be host to the god Anubis.

"Nick Grainger The Curse Of Cleopatra" is the first of three books from Author G.W. Mullins' "Nick Grainger" book series.

FROM THE AUTHOR OF "RISE OF THE SNOW QUEEN - THE POLAR BEAR KING" AND "DANIEL IS WAITING"
THE LEGEND OF
WHITE BEAR
Extended Edition
EVERYONE HAS A BEAST WITHIN THEM...
G.W.
MULLINS

The Legend Of White Bear (Extended Edition)

Nita's tribe faced the coming of the bear every full moon. When it came, many would die.

To protect his daughter, the chief sent her away to live in a rip in time and space, called the void. He told her it was for her protection, but he never told her of the bear history.

One member of his tribe, was burdened with carrying the bear shapeshifter trait. For a lifetime, they would be cursed with being both human and bear until their death. Then a new child would be born to carry the trait.

While in the void, Nita discovers the true horrifying history of the white bear.

Other titles available from G.W. Mullins include:

Timeless - An Adult Paranormal Romance Novel

Aliens, Gods, And Other Paranormal Native
American Tales

The Native American Story Book Volume 1-5-
Stories Of The American Indians For Children

Walking With Spirits Volumes 1-6 Native American
Myths, Legends, And Folklore

The Native American Cookbook

Star People, Sky Gods And Other Tales of The
Native American Indians

More Star People, Sky Gods and Other Paranormal
Tales Of The Native American Indians

For Clarence

"Death smiles at us all, all a man can do is smile back."

— Marcus Aurelius, Roman emperor.

"The boundaries which divide Life from Death are at best shadowy and vague. Who shall say where the one ends, and where the other begins?"

— Edgar Allan Poe

Nuestra Señora de la Santa Muerte, also known as Santa Muerte, is an idol, female deity or folk saint in Mexican and Mexican-American Catholicism. The personification of death, she is believed to be associated with healing, protection, and delivering her devotees safely into the afterlife. Many consider her an Angel of Death.

Before

Jen stepped out of the light, as she orbed into the cemetery. Coming in just near the lake, she looked over to the hill, where the water had washed her down. On the hillside there were still the coffins and the remains of dead body parts. She felt her body tremble in anger as she turned to walk up the hill.

As Jen arrived at the top, she looked over to see Daniel, tied to the stone cross. She smiled, as she mentally sent him the message, "I'm coming." She moved closer and watched, as the fighting there was intense. As she entered the open area, she saw the Black Hat Man, who was walking over to Daniel.

She was not aware if he knew of her presence, but she wanted the element of surprise.

As the demon prepared to strike Daniel again to wake him up, Jen came up from behind. "Get the hell away from him you bastard." Jen walked quickly up to him. The demon was surprised by her appearance, he still believed she was dead. As he looked at her in disbelief, he raised his hand to strike at her. Jen levitated out of his reach, as his arm flew past her.

"What game is this?" He asked.

"It's no game. I've come for Daniel. I suggest you get the hell out of my way."

The demon laughed at her, as he turned away. "What can you do? You are a puny human."

Jen felt the power building within her. As she threw her arms outward, she floated higher, and her body began to glow a bright white light. The demon turned and looked up in fear, as he realized Jen was more of a threat than he ever imagined.

As he began to run, Jen unleashed her full power upon him. The light penetrated his form, and he was raised up into the air. As he shook, his body was being torn apart at a molecular level. With one final wave of power, Jen scattered his body all around the cemetery.

Landing at his feet, Jen reached up and freed Daniel's arm's one at a time. Pulling him close, he buried his head in her shoulder. As Jen held tight, she formed a yellow light around him, that healed and brought him back to full power again.

"I got to save you for once." She laughed at him.

"Yeah, about that. How did you do this?"

"I am a fast learner I guess."

"We have to get the light open. I think I know how to do it." Daniel spoke, as he studied the source of the blockage.

Rising up into the air, Daniel spun around in a circle. The flashing of the blasts in the area, reflected on the skin of his chest as he spun faster. As he threw out his arms and then aimed them upwards, a blast of light stronger than he had ever emitted, flew straight into where the light should have been. The power shook the ground around the cemetery, as the dark figures that clung to the light, fell one by one, disintegrating as they plummeted to the earth below.

Daniel's feet touched the ground again, and he stumbled, trying to get his footing. Jen grabbed him by one arm, as Elizabeth appeared and took the other. They stood and watched, as the tide turned and the dark ones fell. The war would be won that day, but there was one battle left.

"I think we did it." Jen said smiling.

"You did indeed. I am very proud of my students." Elizabeth held tight to both of them.

Muerte had watched the battle from a portal in the underworld. The fighting was over, the dead awaited her. Stepping through space, she appeared in the cemetery.

Within feet of Daniel, she made her presence known. He looked up at her, as she floated down to earth. "Who are you?" He asked in confusion.

"I am someone you once knew. I came to you, when you died decades ago. In a hospital near here I believe." She smiled at him, as she spoke. "I am happy to see such a positive result from claiming a life."

"Thank-you." He responded. "Wait, you are the Angel of Death?"

"Yes, I represent death, and in some cases, life." As she spoke, she waved a hand in front of Daniel, and the last of his wounds healed. "I understand now, why you were chosen. Elizabeth, take care of him, and this remarkable young lady."

Muerte turned and looked down the hill to the direction in which Malachi stood. He looked on in anger, as she approached him. Moving closer, she descended to his side. He turned to look at her with fire in his eyes.

"What that hell are you doing here?" He asked.

"You broke your word, and our contract." She replied. "I have come to collect what is due to me."

"And what would that be?" Malachi turned from her.

Your life belongs to me. You pledged it for one year. Unless you broke the terms of the agreement, and now you are mine in default."

"I belong to no one. You are welcome to try and take me, but I would not advise it. I am a lot stronger than I used to be." Malachi boasted.

"I know, the demon granted you a large amount of power, but be warned, he is no longer here. And as you squander what you have been given, it will not be replaced."

Malachi walked away from her, and extended his arms. A cross-bow and arrow formed within, yielding a darker more powerful version than before.

He did not mean to have to do this twice. He spun around towards Muerte and let go of his energy.

A smile came across her face as Muerte watched the black energy arrow scream towards her. The arrow found its mark deep in the center of her chest. If she still had a heart, it would have shredded on impact. She did not flinch or make a sound, as a release overtook her. She had led this life for more time than she could remember. She embraced her own death, if only for a moment of rest.

Sadly, Muerte knew she would never truly be free of her curse until a successor came. But for the brief time, she would leave her existence. She was grateful. The devastating blow sent her sprawling to the ground. As her body fell, Daniel orbed to her side. "Tell me how to save you!" He shouted.

"I cannot be saved, or lost. I am an entity. Your powers do not work on me." She whispered.

"I saved Elizabeth, let me form a healing shield around you." He pleaded with her.

"It won't work Daniel." Elizabeth spoke from behind him. "She is right, there is nothing we can do. But Malachi, is another subject."

Daniel rose to his feet staring at Malachi. "I have had just about as much of you as I can take."

"I could say the same about you." Malachi snapped back.

They faced each other, as Daniel flexed his arms and brought forth a power buried deep within. Malachi called upon his own rage, and the power bestowed to him. Muerte was right, as Malachi soon realized, his power was weaker every time he used it.

Watching from behind a mausoleum, Raven spread her cloak, and a flock of black birds headed towards Malachi.   He looked up as she shrouded him in darkness. "Come with me, if you want to live." She called out to him.

They both shimmered from sight, reappearing deep in the underworld. "Why did you do that? I can take care of myself."

"He would have killed you. If Abraxas did not stand a chance against them, what makes you think you would. I saved your ass, now we plan our next move. Besides, do you think Muerte is gone for good? She let you win. This is far from over. It is only beginning."

Back in the cemetery, Daniel questioned their win. "What do we do now? If we have won the war, what happens to Jen and myself?" Daniel asked.

"Oh, this is not the end. It's not my choice what happens to you, it's up to him." Elizabeth said pointing upwards. "For now, let's get these guys out of here. Then we have to put this place back the way it was, before the humans know what happened."

"What if the humans have already seen the battle?" Jen asked.

"We will erase the time from everyone's memory."

"What? You can do that?" Daniel asked.

"Well sure, I did it to you. Lots of people have had it done. Just think about the day you swear time got away from you. It probably didn't, we just fixed something." Elizabeth smiled at them.

"Is she telling the truth?" Jen asked.

"Probably, after all we have seen, do you doubt her?"

The last dark figures disappeared from the cemetery, as the three walked forward. Those angels that survived, were taken upwards for healing. The others were gathered for a remembrance ceremony. As Elizabeth walked among the dead, she extended her power, and they floated upwards towards the light. The death count was high, too high in her eyes. She had lost friends, and ones she had known since she left life.

As they were cleared, white lights appeared all around the cemetery. The cleanup crew had arrived. White-Lighters walked the landscape restoring the grounds to the way they looked the moment before the fighting began. Stones were turned back upright or reconstructed. Grass regrew where it had been burned or scorched. The dead bodies that laid strewn all around the grounds, were returned to their coffins and reburied. When they were done, no one could tell anything ever happened.

"And now for the humans." Elizabeth said as she extended her hands, and so did all the other Whitelighters. The immediate area was filled with a white light that entered homes and buildings in the surrounding space. The light filtered through windows, doors and even keyholes. It washed over every living thing for a mile. "And that takes care of the clean-up. It's time to go, it's getting light." With her words, white lights soared upwards to the sky hidden by the morning sun. The only thing that remained was a whisp of shadow from a dark angel.

Mullins

Chapter One: Dark Angel Rising

As Malachi tossed and turned in his bed, his mind raced. There would not be rest that night. He looked upwards to the cavern ceiling, at the jagged rock that covered his view. He wondered how he let this get so far. His life had been uneventful until the night his uncle was dying. He made the choice to call upon Muerte. He had no idea how wrong he was.

As Malachi rolled over in the bed, he closed his eyes for just a minute, he thought. In that time, he drifted into sleep. That is, if sleep were to be misinterpreted as a nightmare. His mind flashed, as darkness moved in front of him. He was stuck in a dark abyss. Strangely it was familiar to him, but he did not know why.

He found himself wondering around, trying to find any light at all, so he could see where he was. He suddenly realized what a blind person must feel like. A panic filled him, as he felt his hands begin to tremble. This place had no real form, it was lifeless and dark.

He continued to try to move, as he heard a humming sound in the distance. His mind raced to identify what he was hearing. It was familiar and almost like a voice of sorts. He leaned his head to the side a bit, and tried to isolate the direction it was coming from.

Moving in the direction of the hum, he was blinded, as a source of light formed near him. It was an orb; he was sure of it. As he squinted, his eyes came into focus. He saw the figure forming in the light. It was Daniel, but how could he be there? This was demonic. An angel would not step foot in the darkness.

"Why are you here?" Malachi spoke, with anger in his voice.

"It's not over you know. Raven may have saved you, but nothing can save you from Muerte." Daniel replied laughing.

"Go to hell angel."

"Hmm, can't you tell? This, is hell. I guess revenge is possible." Daniel said, turning to study the dark place they occupied.

As Daniel moved, his light trailed behind him. With each step, the darkness devoured it. A change took place in his demeanor. The longer he was in the darkness, the less his light emitted. It was as if he was transforming. This place of evil, was consuming anyone there.

"I want out of here. If you got in, you should be able to get us both out. You know the way." Malachi spoke in a desperate voice.

"And why should I help you? Why not call upon your bottom feeder demon, that helped you escape before." Daniel said, with a sinister look upon his face.

"I can't call her. She is out of my reach. I can't leave here on my own."

"So, you need help? Maybe, if you did not kill Muerte, you would have help." Daniel turned and looked away.

"Look, I don't know what game you are playing, or why someone sent me here. I can't leave here without help." Malachi sounded desperate, as his voice cracked and deepened.

Daniel turned back to him. His face had changed, now there was a darkening of his eyes. They were almost black. His blue eyes had faded completely. The brightness of his appearance dimmed. His blond hair washed out, as well as his skin color faded. He was changing before Malachi's eyes.

Malachi thought back, to the transformation he went through, when he became an Angel of Death. The darkness was possessing Daniel in the same way. He drew back in fear of what was happening. If this was true, then Daniel was no longer an angel of the light. With his power darkened, he would be the most dangerous creature in the underworld.

Daniel lowered his head, as he moved toward Malachi. His intentions were not clear, but he radiated evil, as the last of Daniel's light changed to a large black mass of power. As he extended his arms, the darkness engulfed Malachi, and he screamed out in fear.

As Malachi lost his balance, and fell to the ground, the image above him changed. Daniel's form disappeared, in his place a woman stood before Malachi. Her face was drawn and leathery. Her hands were shriveled and looked like a dried corpse. He knew this look; he had seen it before.

Malachi let out a scream, as he knew who he was trapped by. The only word to leave his mouth was, "Muerte." As she moved over his cowering body lying on the floor, she leaned over and formed a wrinkled smile with her shriveled lips. "Did you miss me?"

Back in Malachi's bed, a dark creature of a woman, leaned over his sleeping body. As he thrashed back and forth, she laughed out loud. She took pleasure in his terror. Her form faded, as he was released and woke from his nightmare. Confused, he sat up and whispered, "Muerte."

Chapter Two: She Mostly Comes At Night, Mostly

Malachi sat up in his bed. His head hurt from the dream that was forced into his sleep. He rubbed his eyes hoping for some relief. It was a futile gesture, nothing seemed to help. Only time, would release the pressure in his head.

Standing up, he pulled up his pants, but did not bother to button them. He knew there was no one in the cavern. With Muerte gone, he was alone…in the cavern and in the underworld. At first, he thought that was a good thing. Then he realized, he was one of the weaker creatures in the food chain.

He made his way to the outer hall, and found the viewing portal, Muerte had taught him to use. He reached out a hand to swirl the mists, but as he was about to speak, he felt hands, sliding around from his back and up his sides. The feeling was nice at first, then unsettling. He stopped breathing for a second, wondering who had run their hands up his chest and stomach.

Taking a deep breath, he quickly grabbed ahold of the hands, and pulled them from his body, as he spun around. As he came face to face with the woman behind him, he let loose a sigh of relief. She was not a threat, just a low-level demon.

"Raven! What are you doing here?" He asked

"I came to be with my sexy young boy. Is that a crime?" She said, trying to make an innocent face.

"First of all, I am not your anything. And yes, anything you have planned or are doing, is usually a crime." He growled, as he turned back to the portal.

"So, the poor little whipping boy, is missing his mistress?" She laughed.

"I assure you, I am missing no one. Well, maybe, myself. The person I used to be. I want to go back to my family and friends. I want my freedom." He sulked.

"My boy, you have freedom, power and can do whatever you want, now that the wicked witch of the west had a house fall on her."

"Yeah, my house fell on her, and now I am stuck with this darkness flowing through my veins. I mean, look at me. I look like a zombie. You can see it through my skin. These dark veins run all over my body." He stared into the mist, as his words trailed off.

"I am afraid no one can remove the darkness, except for an Angel of Death. That seems to be something we are in short supply of these days. You are it babe. Until another comes along." Raven tried to comfort him, but he pulled away from her touch.

"Ok, I get the hint. I am not wanted here, and I do not stay where I am not wanted." Raven stepped backwards, as she shimmered into a distorted image and disappeared.

"Finally!" He huffed, and his attention went back to the portal.

He thought back to the first days he was there. He remembered catching Muerte looking into the portal.

~~~~~~~

Santa Muerte stood looking through her portal into the past. She thought about her new apprentice. She watched as he slept. Her mind raced to when she was still human. Moving her hand over the portal, she saw the mist change within, the images went back to the time of 1847. The Mexican-American war raged through Texas. She stared on, until she saw herself.

"Mi amor, I promise this is not what I planned for you in life. Please, no matter what happens, remember mama loved you so much. If I could have
~~~~~~~

changed this, I would have. I just do not know how to save you, or myself."

As Carlotta finished speaking, she heard the soldiers making their way down the side street. She pulled Anna close and covered her mouth. "Do not cry, do not make a sound." She whispered, as the door began to open slowly.

As the soldier studied her, he did not care for her or her child. This man was more interested in what trophies he could claim. People were little more than animals to him. He raised his rifle into the air. A smile crossed his lips, as he prepared to claim another notch for his collection of kills. The shot rang out, as Anna watched her mother fall sideways on the ground.

She stood looking at her mother and screaming, as the soldier reloaded his rifle. "Don't worry, it will be over soon." He said, laughing at Anna.

She stood there watching, paralyzed by her own fear. Santa Muerte yelled at her, "Why don't you run and hide. Just save yourself." She raised her hands to her head, as the sound of the rifle firing, rang through the room. Clutching her chest, she caressed the point where the bullet had hit her. If she still had a heart, she thought it would hurt.

A few feet away, the dark shadow came. As it moved forward, it took shape. Soon, a man emerged from within the darkness. Dressed in black from head to toe, he wore a dress suit and looked like an undertaker. "So many dead, so many souls to claim. I'll be here a while." The Angel of Death was pleased.

He made his way down the street, until finding the bodies of Carlotta and Anna. Looking down at Anna, he shook his head. "Little One, you never had a chance in life, did you?"

As he lifted Anna into his arms, he carried her through the streets. His pain was obvious, as he struck out at those who caused the death of such a young girl. In moments, he killed all who were in the immediate area, before lifting himself upwards with the child still in his arms.

In his own realm, he took Anna to his private chamber. There he took a small amount of his power, and formed a ball of energy in front of him. Looking down at the girl, he aimed his hand, shooting the power within her. "My child, forgive me for what I do, but this is the only way I know to give you life again." With the power surging through her, she took a deep breath, and sat up coughing.

"Arise Muerte. My child, born of death."

"My name is Anna." She said staring at him.

"You were…Anna, now you are so much more. You are…the Queen of the Dead."

As his words echoed through the room, Malachi watched from behind. He had been there the whole time. He understood a little better what was happening. He had enlisted his soul with that of the dead.

Malachi looked on in disbelief, as the history of Muerte unfolded. With a wave of her hand,

Muerte cleared the view portal. She sighed, as she turned away, to see Malachi sitting behind, his fear showing like a beacon. She knew instantly he had seen her.

"You were human once." He spoke, trembling. "What will you ask of me? What am I expected to do?"

"You will go forth and prepare the dead, in different times and places. I will choose the place, and you will ready people, for me to claim."

"What do you mean times?"

"The living, believe in such linear lives. Not everything goes forward in the line of time. In truth, time is irrelevant. Living outside of time, we can move backwards and forwards at will. The dead have to be claimed. If they were not, then hell on earth, would be a real thing."

Muerte walked the hall, passing one empty room after another. As she floated past, she glanced into them. Inside, as she watched, a scene came to life. There, wars played out, as did natural disasters.

As Malachi followed, his vision changed. His eyes darkened to a point; the images of death were clear to him.

Muerte turned to him, and looked him in the eyes. "Your transformation has given you the gift of after-sight. Now you will see, what the dead see. If someone is dying, you will be able to see the change and the approach of death. One day, you will learn to hate what has been thrust upon you. Do not let it rob the humanity you have left."

Chapter Three: The Portal Into The Past

Malachi moved a hand towards the portal. Cautiously, he moved his fingers into the mist and changed the way it swirled. He thought of his intent and where he wanted to go. "I could change this, if I wanted to." He spoke as if someone was listening. "I could turn back time and reset all that happened."

He thought long and hard, about what event he would have to change, to recover his humanity. He realized it was dangerous to tamper with the past, but Muerte said time was different than humans believed. He was sure he had no choice, but to try to go back.

Malachi thought hard, before realizing, it was the night he called upon Muerte. If he could stop the accident or prevent himself from calling for help, then everything would go back to normal. He mustered his courage, as he turned back time and looked into his own past.

As he stepped through the portal, the rain began to pelt his face. The storm was strong. As he looked around, he thought the storm was different. This was no normal event. It was engineered.

Raising his hand, to shield his eyes that stung from the rain, he saw the car the he and his uncle were in, coming out of control. As he stood there, Malachi realized the car was aiming at him. If he did not do something, he would be run over.

Pulling his arms back, he unleashed a blast of dark energy in the direction of the car. The violence of the storm masked his assault. As his power hit, the car began to flip and roll. It was then, Malachi stepped back in terror. He wondered if the accident was his fault. Had he traveled back before, and caused this same event?

He fell to his knees, as he realized there was nothing he could do. He doubled over in pain, as he knew there was no way to fix anything.

As Malachi looked to the ground, he did not see the light, which cut through the sky. It was bright, and filled the area, as it landed just behind him. The figure of a man stepped out, and stood staring at him. He looked on in disbelief, at what was occurring.

"It wouldn't have worked." The blond man walked over.

"Daniel! What the hell, are you doing here?"

"The Guardians have a way of monitoring the timeline. When you traveled back, you caused a ripple in time. They sent me to stop whatever you thought you were trying to do. I think I understand. You want to go back." Daniel called out, over the rain and thunder.

"It didn't do me much good, did it? I am stuck this way. I will never get my life back."

Daniel walked over to him, and kneeled on the pavement. "Maybe there is some other way. I have seen so much, since I became an angel. Impossible things, crazy things that should not be possible. Let us help you."

"I tried to kill you, on more than one occasion, not to mention your girlfriend. Why would I expect your help?" Malachi asked.

"I would do it, because it is who I am. I wouldn't expect as much out of Jen…she would kill you. She's a little hot headed. If you want help, you just have to ask."

"If I thought it would do any good, I would ask, but the darkness in me won't let go. It is already trying to make me attack you. I don't know how long I can hold it off. Maybe you should leave." Malachi said, as he struggled to get to his feet.

Daniel stepped back, he knew the darkness was in control, and Malachi had no choice. He formed an orb and prepared to leave, as he looked on to the car, where the past version of Malachi was looking for his uncle. Shaking his head, Daniel climbed upward.

Malachi moved out of view, and watched from a distance, as history played out. He ran the scene through his brain, time and again, with no resolution. It all had to happen, and nothing in his power could change the past.

As he watched, he knew the outcome, and soon Muerte would be called forward. That was one thing, even he, did not want to hang around for. He moved down the street, and returned to the portal that had brought him there.

After stepping through, the mist began to clear. He felt crushed by the mistake he had made. Turning back to the portal, he was sure he saw something, moving just beyond the last layer of the mist. As he moved toward it, a dried skeletal looking hand reached through, grabbing him by the throat.

"Did you think a mere apprentice could kill me…boy?" A voice called from the portal.

Chapter Four: Shadows Of The Past

Malachi fell backwards, as the hand turned loose from his throat. He gasped for air, as he thrashed back and forth, trying to get back on his feet. He felt the queasy sick feeling in his head, as if he was about to throw up. Nothing had prepared him for this level of fear.

He screamed out for help, but no one was there to save him. He was alone in the underworld. Stranded in the world of demons, by his own hands and mistakes. Nothing or no one could save him.

Far above Malachi, in the Upper Realm, Elizabeth stared into the pool before her. She observed him, trying to make sense of what he was doing. She shook her head in disbelief.

"How could you go so off path?" she whispered.

"He was not prepared for all that was thrown at him." Daniel replied, as he walked in behind her.

"I saw you went to him. You knew he would not listen." She sighed.

"I had to try. There is something about him. I feel like he has to be saved." Daniel tried to explain, as he stared in the pool.

They both turned to the back of the room, as Jen orbed in. She stepped forth from the light, looking confused by their concern. "What's up?" She asked. "You guys were really distracted."

"Malachi…need I say anymore?" Elizabeth groaned.

"He's in trouble. I just feel like he needs help." Daniel looked back at the pool.

"Turn me loose, I will give him something to think about. I mean, after all, his acts led to my death."

"Well, he had a little help." Elizabeth added.

"Still, I don't believe this was his intended path. Can we back up the window, and see a time when he was still human?" Daniel asked.

"Yes, but I don't understand what you are looking for." She spoke, as the waters of the pool swirled.

"There, slow down and let his life play out."

As they watched, Malachi appeared as a human, much younger in age. He had just lost his parents. He was with is Uncle, dealing with his loss. That night, when he went to bed, he folded his hands in prayer.

As he fell into a deep exhausted sleep, he was unaware of anything around him. Curled up with his pillow, he did not see a light entering the room. The bright yellow color of the light, washed over everything. The light scanned the room, exploring, to make sure it was safe.

Then a form exited the light. It was a man, but no mere man…an angel. His skin glowed, as he walked forward. He moved to the side of Malachi's bed, observing the young boy as he slept. Opening his lips, he spoke. "Don't worry young one. I will take care of you."

"Who the hell is that?" Elizabeth said in confusion.

"He's an angel, but I have never seen him before. What is he doing there?" Jen replied.

Daniel watched and studied him. "He's not one of us. Was Malachi supposed to be a Charge?"

"I'll check." Elizabeth studied the records of all the protected ones in the time period. "Oh Daniel, this can't be right. He was no Charge, he was destined."

"How can that be? He is a demon." Jen's voice rose.

"We will find out. Obviously, somehow, he fell through the cracks. But then again, who is the angel?" Elizabeth watched the man, as he sat down beside Malachi and took his hand.

The angel looked at the boy, as he reached his other hand towards Malachi's head. As he made contact, a light began to engulf them both. As the light spread, the boy began to jerk. His body reacted as if he were having a seizure.

"What the hell is he doing to Malachi?" Elizabeth grew concerned.

"It looks like he is taking control. We have to look into this. Can you send me back to that time, just a few minutes before he arrives?" Daniel looked hard at Elizabeth.

"Yes, when you are prepared, let me know."

"Do it."

Chapter Five: Fallen Angel

Daniel stood silently, as the past washed over him. At first, the winds swirled, and showed him the last few minutes playing backwards. Then, he began to travel back by years at a time. He had time-traveled before, but not intentionally. He remembered the last time, when he was thrown backwards through time. Only to end up the pawn of an evil demon, who terrorized him in a Nazi prison camp.

Daniel flinched, as he remembered the pain he endured, at the hands of Abraxas. He was almost killed, as he had no power to leave the place. If Elizabeth had not opened a doorway to save him, he would have died in the gas chamber which Abraxas ordered him into. With that thought, he did not feel so bad, that Jen obliterated him.

Daniel felt the movement, as the years slowed, and he neared his destination. He watched, as Malachi laid his head on the pillow. The blue light filled the room, as Daniel stepped forward, quickly finding a hiding place in the closet, where he could watch and wait.

In minutes, the angel appeared and went to the bed side. Daniel studied the man and his face. Something was not right about this. He was behaving like no angel Daniel had seen before. They were not supposed to control an innocent's body.

Daniel emerged from the closet. "Whatever you are doing, you need to stop now."

The angel turned and faced him. "Who are you?"

"Funny, I was about to ask you the same thing. Let go of the boy, and answer my question." Daniel demanded.

"I am a guardian angel. I am here to care for the boy." The man spoke, as he trembled.

"Funny, I am an angel, but I am not so sure about you."

The angel spun around and attempted to orb away. Daniel was prepared, and erected a shield, just as the man's feet lifted from the floor. A smile crossed Daniel's face, as he pulled the man back down.

"You weren't going to get away that easily." Daniel said confidently. "Now let's try this again. Who are you?"

"I am Emil, I am Malachi's father." He answered.

"There is no record of you being an angel. Malachi's parents died in an accident, and then nothing."

"That's where it gets complicated. My wife was human, I was an angel. An angel who fell from grace. I was outcast, and then I found Lacey. We fell in love and conceived a son. She did not know I was not human. I didn't even know we could have a child. It shouldn't even be possible. Then Malachi was born. I had to let everyone think I died." He hung his head in embarrassment.

In the Upper Realm, Elizabeth and Jen continued to watch. "What kind of crazy is this?" Jen asked.

"Tell me about it, this is too much." Elizabeth said taking a deep breath.

"Well, I have to admit, I did not see this coming." Jen shook her head, and looked down.

Back in the bedroom, Daniel walked circles around the man. He had no idea what to think, or how to handle the situation. He did not sense deception, but something about all this bothered him.

"Ok, if he is your son, what were you doing to him?" Daniel showed his frustration in his voice.

"I have visited him, to try to erase parts of his memory of myself and his mother. I figured if his memories were gone or buried, he might not suffer as much. I want him to have a better life without the pain." The man said, as tears filled his eyes.

"I don't know if this was the right choice. The pain we suffer and the experiences we retain from life, make us who we are. If you take away a part of that, then you might change him forever. Maybe that is part of the reason for the choices he made." Daniel stopped short in his response.

"Wait, you are not from this time, are you?" Emil asked.

"No, I am not."

"You are from his future, aren't you? What do you know? Tell me…I sense you are holding back something!" Emil demanded.

"I cannot tell you the future. If I did, then your choices, might change what has happened. We don't need a paradox. The whole future might be changed by the simplest of things." Daniel struggled to explain.

"You mean change a simple thing, like you being here now?" Emil snapped.

"No, as long as he does not see you or me, we are fine. As an angel, you are outside of time and space. I just wonder if what you are doing, has an effect later about choices he has made."

"If we cannot change the past, can we correct something I have done, in the future. If I traveled forward with you, could I then give him back the things I have taken?" He said, looking down at his child.

"Perhaps, but you may not like what you find in the future."

"If I can save him, I will do what I have to."

Daniel looked down, at the innocent boy Malachi had been. He knew if there was a way to save him, he had to try. Daniel reached out, and touched the man's shoulder. Emil looked down to say goodbye to his son, as the boy began to awaken. Quickly, Daniel pulled Emil into the light, as he began to drag him forward in time.

As they disappeared, Malachi sat up in his bed, to see the flashing blue light that filled the room.

He called out to his uncle, who came running. 'What is it mijo?"

"The blue lights, they were all around my room. What was it?" Malachi asked.

"I see nothing young one. Perhaps a police car drove by with its lights on, and they filled the room. Your curtains are open after all."

Malachi looked at the window and cocked his head. "Maybe, that was all it was. Goodnight, Uncle."

As Carl left the room, he fell back against the wall. He closed his eyes. He hated the lying. He knew the truth, but he could not bring Malachi into the crazy existence, he was forced to live for years. He had promised Lacey to keep the secret, and he would honor his sister's memory.

Mullins

.

Chapter Six: The Dead Awaken

The gloomy darkened hallways of the underworld, set the scene for the existence of evil. There was not much light, or anything to promote a feeling of good. The place reeked of odd smells and bad feelings. The environment, was perfect for the likes of demons and creatures of the night.

The place, did not make Malachi feel any better about himself. The darkness within him, fed off his surroundings. He struggled within himself to retain any of his humanity. Deep down, he knew he was not, what the energy coursing through his veins wanted.

Malachi knew he had to find light, and a place to regain his hold. He had to return to the surface. Sadly, the only place he had a familiarity with was the cemetery. Even though it was the scene of so much turmoil, it was still a place he could control the darkness.

He shimmered out of sight, and transported to the area of the cemetery, where the lake had just begun to settle, after the battle they had forced upon it. He looked around himself. The grounds looked calm and normal. There were no signs of the destruction. The angels had cleaned the place well. He smiled with a secret joy, in the power he had unleased with Abraxas.

No, he thought, it was not anything to be proud of. Lives were taken there. Luckily, the only human to die, was Jen. His heart sank, as he thought of her. He admired the girl and her beauty. Maybe he thought, that was one of the reasons he disliked Daniel. He wanted to be like him, but there was little he could do, to change who he was.

Malachi walked along, looking at the stones of the cemetery, all the while feeling the sun on his skin. The lake, had pulled back into the shape it was intended to have. The washed over area from the flooding, was drying looking as it once did. Even though the place was meant for the dead; he felt a liking for it. It was not just for the dead to inhabit.

As Malachi walked along, he spotted something out of the corner of his eye. A familiar stone. One he had seen before. He thought back to when he was a child. He had been here, but why? It seemed, so much of his memory, had been hidden from him. It was confusing, like a person with a form of amnesia.

As he came to the stone, he planted his foot against it, as he kneeled down. He looked at the name and drew back in shock. Lacey, it was his mother's name. He sat back in confusion. He had been there before; he just could not reach the memory of the event, or even his mother's death. He just needed a trigger, to bring her death back to mind.

With a single word, he opened his mouth. "Mom?" Then, he folded his arms around his knees, as he sat there on the damp ground. He searched himself for the memories that had been locked away from him. Like looking into a room that you could not go into, he felt the events of his past that had been taken away, and he grew angry.

A light rain fell over his head, as he searched his memories, for all the locked doors that lay before him. "How is this possible?" He whispered to himself. "Who did this to me?"

As he reached out for the tombstone that marked his mother's grave, a slight shock of energy shot through his hand. It was electrical, perhaps from the storm that was about to happen. Maybe a charge of static electricity. Or maybe, something more that he did not understand.

As he sat there trying to understand more than he should have had to face, he felt a presence near him. Something or someone familiar, was coming into existence. The darkness within him stirred at such a force of light. It feared the effect this presence had over him.

Malachi looked up and studied the area. As he looked upwards, the rain filled his eyes and stung as if it were burning him. He struggled to climb to his feet, as the light filled the area all around. Whatever was causing it, had grown closer. He felt the result, from his head down to his feet. He wanted to run, but knew he had to stay and confront whatever this was.

"It is OK my little one. I have not come to hurt you. You know, I always loved you." The voice echoed through his head.

"Who are you?" He called out.

"Someone, who has missed you so much."

The voice was female, and very familiar to him. He had not heard it in so long. The memories he had of it, were from childhood and had been left a decade behind him. The other memories, were locked in the vault, in his head. He knew this woman. She was so comforting, just by familiarity.

Then one word came from his lips. "Mama."

Chapter Seven: Sins of the Father

Lacey's spirit grew closer, as Malachi felt the lump growing in his throat. So many emotions filled his head. He felt like a child who wanted to run to his mother. And then, there was the feeling of anger, followed by grief. He felt as if his life was crashing in on him. He had been betrayed, and that much he was sure of.

He watched as Lacey took form in front of him. Tears ran from his face, as he saw the woman he remembered from when he was a child. As he ran through his memories, he realized how much was no longer available to him. Somehow, many of his years had holes in them. Then he wondered, who could have done this to him.

The angels would never do this as an act of revenge, it wasn't their style. Abraxas had no need to control him, neither did Raven for that matter. There had to be someone closer to the source. His mind turned to Muerte. Maybe, as she needed to control him, but what would this accomplish?

As tears streamed down, his mother moved in close, and ran a hand across his face to remove them. "My love, you were always an emotional child." She said, smiling at him.

"Mama, I don't understand. You have been dead so long. Why have you come to me now?' He asked.

"Because you needed me. And, because I don't get the opportunity to do this much. There are rules in death. I couldn't say goodbye to you before, so I am here to see you now." Lacey chose her words carefully, being she was trying to make sense of what had happened to her son.

"You are staring at me. I guess, I am not what you expected, after all this time." He tried to find his words.

"You are older yes, but this darkness that flows inside you. Where did it come from?"

"I made a mistake and gave my life to save uncle Carl. Mama he was dying and I had no choice, so I called on Santa Muerte. She said if I gave her a year of my life, she would save him. He is well now, but I am trapped. She turned me into this, and I killed her. Now I am stuck in this existence."

"If she made a contract, even with her death, shouldn't you return to your old self?" She asked.

"Only if she were here to release me. I screwed up so badly. I don't want to be an Angel of Death." He hung his head, as his words disappeared.

"If you prayed for help from Muerte, then a prayer for help from the angels, might help as well. Whatever you do my love, do not let the darkness take away your light. Whatever you did, I doubt was enough to kill Muerte. If she was an Angel of Death, then she cannot be killed easily."

Malachi looked up at her and smiled. She had lightened his heart. For the moment, he was in control over the darkness. As he looked at his mother, his eyes lightened for a moment. He almost looked normal.

"Mother, do you know of anyone who could tamper with my memory? There is so much, that has been taken away from me. So much, a normal person could not do." He asked her.

"Maybe it is time, we had a talk about your father." She said caressing his cheek. "Your father was not who you thought he was."

"You mean, he was another man?"

"No, the man you knew, was really your father. He was just different." She said as she turned away, harboring the secret she did not want to tell. "Your father was not human."

"I don't understand. What was he?"

"He was and angel, and your birth was not supposed to be allowed." She choked on her words.

"Are you kidding me? You mean, I am half angel? How in the hell is that even possible?" He screamed.

"We loved each other. It was…what it was. We tried to keep our secret, but the Guardians found out. Back then, it just wasn't done. No one, knew what the child of such a union would be. Your father was my Guardian Angel, and I was his Charge. It just happened. We never intended to fall in love, or even have a child." She tried to tell him the story, while leaving out things he did not need to know.

"And when they found out? Was that how you died?" He grew angrier with each word.

"No, they had nothing to do with my death. They protected us, and our secret. They even erased all history of your father, so the newer generations of angels would not even know either of us existed. I died in an accident. There was nothing they could do to save me."

"Why didn't they make you an angel as well? They did that to someone who died recently. I know it to be real."

"You can only become an angel, if you are destined. You have to be in line for it, have a reason. Unless, some demon took your life, before you had lived past the point you were meant to. I was a mere mortal, who lived her life to a destined end."

"Then where is my father?" He demanded.

Chapter Eight: Reunited In Death

"Just tell me, where the hell he is." Malachi had passed his point of anger.

"I am here." Emil's voice rang in from behind.

As Daniel and Emil stepped out of the light, Malachi turned to them. Anger filled his eyes, as the darkness returned. He struggled to find words, as he realized his whole life had been filled with lies. It all ran through his brain, before he gained control of his thoughts.

"You lied to me. About who you were. About my life." His voice got louder, with every word. "Wait, did Carl know about all of this? Was he in on your lies?"

"No, he did not know in the beginning. He figured it out only recently, as he walked in, as I was watching you sleep." Emil tried to stay calm and choose his words carefully. "No one, intended to lie to you. It was for your own protection. After your mother died, I could not risk anything happening to you. I made a bad decision, in letting you think I died as well."

"Really…do you think so? I guess that tombstone next to my mother, is just a symbol of the fake death you had?" Malachi's voice went hoarse from his screaming.

"Son, I had to do what I thought was right. I never wanted this life for you. I did not want you to know of the fight between good and evil. I never wanted you to know what a demon was."

"Take a good look father, I think I figured it out." Malachi said, turning away.

"I made mistakes." Emil whispered. "Bad mistakes. Daniel convinced me of that. He made sense of all of this. I came here to make this right. Somehow."

"If I had only known, I would have never called upon Muerte. I could have saved Carl myself. Daniel...I had powers like you all along, didn't I?"

Daniel stepped forward in shock. He did not want to come between their fight. "Yes, there is a good chance you have dormant powers. If you had known of them, they might have surfaced by now."

"But, no one told me what I was. So, I did the best I knew how to. I saved his life by making a contract, that I really never had to do."

"Malachi, allow me to give back, what I took away over so many years. It can be a first step in making this right." Emil said, extending his hand.

"What are you going to do?" Malachi tried to understand.

"I will release the memory locks, I put in place, since you were a child."

"What will that do to me?"

"It will give you back a lifetime of memories, that you were robbed of." Emil spoke, as he placed a hand on Malachi's head, and emitted a glowing light.

As Malachi regained his memories, his eyes filled with tears, and he let go of a sound of torture, that emitted from his throat. So much sensory overload filled him, as he saw a lifetime of family and his parents. His body shook as his brain traveled through time, and he saw all the love his parents had for him.

Then, as he was coming to terms with the pain and anger, he relived their deaths. This time, he knew his father never died. His mother, was there to comfort him, as he saw her death. She wrapped her arms around him, and poured out all the love she could give.

Malachi looked around in confusion. He did not know what to do. He wanted to hate his father, but the memories that returned, gave him reason to try to understand. And then, there was his mother. His heart ached for her and how she died. She was but a spirit now. There was no bringing her back from the dead.

"Where do we go from here? Mama, where are you, when you are not here with me?" Malachi asked.

"In the spirit realm. It is a place we all go after death. There are friends and family. Your father has spent much time with me there." She said smiling.

"He's not dead. How can he go there?"

"He is an angel, it is allowed. It is how we stayed together, since my death." Lacey tried to explain.

"And since you were destined to be an angel…maybe one day, you could go there to visit too." Daniel explained.

"But not while I am an Angel of Death. That's what you left out." Malachi sounded defeated.

"We will find a way to fix this. For now, you are fully aware of your memories and your life. It's a starting point." Emil tried to comfort him.

"Malachi, I have to leave you now. My time on this plane is limited. But soon, I will return to you, and we will see each other again. Please forgive your father, and let him be with you. He is a powerful angel, and he can help. If you let him." She started to disappear, as she finished speaking.

"I love you always." He said back to her, as she disappeared.

"I don't know where to go from here. I don't want to go back to the underworld." Malachi sounded desperate.

"Then do not go there. It is your choice." Daniel said, just as a dark mist entered the cemetery.

"What the hell is going on?" Emil screamed as the winds surrounded them, like a hurricane.

"This is not natural in origin." Daniel called back.

Above, Jen and Elizabeth watched, as the portal formed around them in the cemetery. The darkness grew and moved towards Malachi. His eyes grew large, as he knew what was about to happen.

Someone in the Underworld had sent a portal. They were trying to take him. But who? Only one person was capable of activating the gateways, and she was dead.

Chapter Nine: Out Of The Darkness

Malachi opened his mouth to scream, as he felt his feet being dragged into the swirling darkness. Daniel threw himself forward, grabbing ahold of Malachi's hand. He pulled backwards, as he attempted to orb. As light came forward from his body, and it started to engulf the both of them. The light moved down Malachi's body, meeting the darkness of the demonic light, and Daniel's light faded.

"Why isn't this working?" Daniel moaned, as he struggled to hold onto Malachi.

"Pull harder!" Malachi screamed, as he held tight, and he felt his body being dragged away.

As Jen watched through the viewer, she knew she had to take action. She didn't care for Malachi, but she would not let Daniel come to harm. Backing away from Elizabeth, she orbed before any questions could be asked.

As Jen appeared behind Daniel, she grabbed his arm and pulled as hard as she could. "I'm getting good at saving you. I think we traded places." As she extended her light and pulled, she felt her feet slipping forward. Turning to Daniel, she looked him in the eyes. They both knew they were about to lose this battle.

The darkness absorbed his body, and Malachi began to move into the portal. It did not take long before he was dragged in completely, along with his rescuers. The three fell downward into the underworld, crashing onto the floor.

Malachi hit hard, slamming his head against the stone wall. He struggled to retain consciousness, as blood streamed down his forehead. He looked to see Daniel and Jen, who fell just behind him. His vision went in and out of focus as he blinked his eyes.

As Jen struggled to get to her feet, she pressed her hands to the dirty stone floor. She emitted a light to see what she was touching. It would be something she would regret for some time. The floor was covered with an oily thick substance, she was sure was excrement. She jumped up quickly and emitted a glow from her hands, burning the substance from her skin.

"What disgusting place have we been dragged to?" She said, not trying to hide her revulsion.

"Welcome to the underworld." Malachi said, as he tried to hold back the stream of blood from his head.

"Hold still, and I will try to heal you." Daniel said, as he leaned over him.

"I thought that kind of thing, did not work on demons and bad guys like me." Malachi laughed, as he spoke.

"It's not supposed to, but it seems we have learned, you are more than a bad guy." Daniel spoke, as he moved his hand over the wound.

A yellow healing light emerged from him, as Daniel looked on at his handy work. The blood slowed and the wound began to close. Soon, the blood began to disappear, and Malachi felt his balance returning. Daniel smiled at him, pleased he was able to help.

"You are always the golden boy, aren't you?" Malachi asked.

"What? He healed you, and you still come across as a jerk." Jen was angry, and had no trouble showing it.

"Calm down sweetheart. I meant no harm. The darkness is still in here. I guess I will have to work on controlling it."

"I would, before she hurts you." Daniel laughed.

"Point taken. I apologize."

"So, where are we?" Jen growled.

"I have no idea. I know we are in the underworld, but as to where, I have no idea." Malachi said, looking around.

"We need to get out of here. This is no place for Whitelighters. I am sure the demons are aware of our presence." Daniel added.

"Hmmm…blond, beautiful and he is smart." A female voice came from the darkness.

As she stepped into the light, Malachi stared hard. Raven had returned, and as usual, she was scheming to get attention in the underworld hierarchy. Malachi walked towards her, shaking his head. He did not take her seriously. "What the hell do you think you are doing?" He asked.

"I would say, taking hostages and gaining power."

"You think one low level demon can take me and two Whitelighters?" he said, staring into her eyes.

"Oh, sweet boy, I am not doing this alone. I am not that foolish. I brought friends." She laughed. "Boys come in, and say hello."

As she turned and waved her hand, behind her four demonic creatures took form. Their appearance was inhuman, with red skin and hornlike objects forming out of their heads. Their bodies sported muscle, that any weightlifter would envy.

Raven turned to smile at Malachi. "Will they do?"

"Why are you doing this? You wanted to work with me." He pleaded with her.

"Things change. People change. Let's say, I found a better offer." She raised a hand, and stroked his cheek. "I don't need you anymore. Shame."

As Raven pulled her fingers away from his face, she slapped Malachi. A sinister smile covered her face, as she moved out of the way. "Boys, you know what to do."

The demons surrounded them as they grabbed ahold of Jen's arms. As Jen struggled, a blast of visions flooded her mind. "I know you. You were the one at the beach, who sent that dark water creature after me. You were going to kill me."

"Oh, how sweet, she remembers me." Raven mocked her.

Jen's mind raced back, as she relived the day by the sea, and the moment she was attacked. Her anger grew, as she traveled backwards, to a moment where she was totally defenseless. She struggled to take a deep breath, surrounded by the foul smells and gas.

~~~~~~

As Jen left Daniel's side and went to the light house door, above on the observation deck, Raven had been watching the whole event transpire. She walked back inside and turned to the dark water creature. "I have one more thing I want you to do for now. I gave you power, now mama needs a favor. The girl at the bottom of the stairs needs to die. Can
~~~~~~

you do that for mama?" Raven smiled, as the creature acknowledged her and walked towards the stair case.

As it made its way down, Jen looked around the lower level. There wasn't much there, just a few old machine parts, and a power unit that fed the light above. As Jen turned her back to the steps, the creature moved quickly behind her. She turned to go back to the door, as it latched on to her arm and threw her against the wall. Jen fought back as hard as she could, but a human was no match for a creature with power. As he tossed her back and forth, the last blow he gave, threw her backwards into the power unit.

Sparks flew as the unit exploded, sending Jen flying across the room and against the floor. She didn't know what had hit her, before it was too late. Another innocent life had been taken.

As Jen's life faded, Raven approached from the stairs. She walked over to her dark creature, and touched his shoulder. "You have done well. I am very pleased with you today. Now go and hide, while I attend to our friend here."

The creature acknowledged her, and disappeared into the dark corner of the room. Raven walked over and looked at Jen. As she touched Jen's hair, she admired her beauty and youth. Raven had neither, she was hundreds of years old, and only maintained herself, by claiming power from lower forms of demons. "You were a pretty one, weren't you? It is a pity you had to die this way, but it is all for the grander scheme of things you know. We all have to do our part."

As Raven stood back up, she saw the signs of the Shadow approaching. Jen's body shook and then her eyes opened, as her head flew back. Raven walked circles around the event as it happened. She admired the Shadow's handy work. They were so much more powerful than she was.

"Hello. Come to join the party I see." Raven joked.

"Lower demon scum, what are you up to?" The Shadow asked.

"I just left you a gift is all. I knew you would have to find someone near Daniel to occupy, so I made it easy for you. Shall we say, I helped you?"

"This is no gift; you have compromised the order. We cannot take a life that is not meant to die and use it for our bidding."

"You didn't…I did. Well, the dark water creature I freed from his captivity did. So, you could say, we are both in the clear. We are merely innocent by-standers."

"There is nothing innocent about you…demon." The Shadow growled.

"That may be true, but I handed you a gift. Now you can use it to claim the boy for your own."

"And what do you get from all this?"

Raven laughed. "Nothing, which is exactly what the side of good will get. They don't get any stronger, and the dark is growing already. It is still a win for my side. Now, go and claim your prize. I don't think Daniel will fight back much now."

~~~~~~

Jen emerged from her vision, and she was angry. Her eyes began to glow, as the creature, threw her into the cell that awaited them. As the door closed, Jen raised her head, and prepared to unleash a power buried deep within her. As a young girl she had always been told to bury her anger deep down and never let it show. Those days were over. Her whole body began to glow as she turned loose her anger.
~~~~~~

Chapter Ten: Welcome To The Underworld

Jen felt the power building within. Her hands tingled, as she raised them, aiming at the dark figure Raven, who stood there taunting her. Jen's memories fueled the fire inside. She remembered the hurt, and the creature who tried to take her life. Today, she thought, she would have justice.

Daniel moved to the side; he knew what was about to happen. He knew what she was capable of. He also knew she was new to her abilities. That in itself, scared him.

Jen felt her power reach its peak, and she aimed her force at Raven. Pulling back her hands, she allowed the force to emerge. Just as Jen started to send her energy, a smug look covered Raven's face. Then the force of Jen's blast faded.

Jen turned to Daniel, who watched in disbelief. "What the hell happened?" She asked.

"Oh, it's simple my dear. I brought a friend along, for just such an occasion."

Then Raven turned and gestured towards the shadows in the side of the filth covered hallway. As Jen looked deep into the darkness, she saw movement. It was slow at first, then the silhouette came into the light. The shape took form, showing its dark slimy skin. It was the dark water creature.

Jen felt a lump form in her throat. She felt like she wanted to throw up. She never thought she would see him again. His presence was surely not a good one. Jen just stood, moving her fingers, trying to regain her power. But nothing came.

"You can try that all day, it will not work. You see, my handsome creature has blocked your abilities. As long as he is here, you can do nothing." Raven laughed; she was enjoying the power she had over the situation. "Boys, if you would kindly take our guests to their cell."

The demons surrounded them, and took each one forcefully. One of the demons grabbed hard to Jen, and she returned the favor by elbowing hard into his ribs. The show of force had no effect. The large muscular creature seemed devoid of feelings.

As they were thrown into the carved room, the demons erected a cage door made of energy behind them. Just outside, the dark water creature stood staring at Jen. He studied her. It was as if he remembered her from before. He moved his eyes over every inch of her body.

Jen felt a disgust, as the creature seemed to take pleasure in watching her. She turned away and looked to the others, who had also noticed the creature. Daniel placed a hand on Jen's back to comfort her, which seemed to make the creature upset. A sad moaning sound seemed to be coming from him, like a child showing unhappiness.

"Daniel, he doesn't like it when you touch Jen." Malachi whispered.

"Yes, I noticed that too. Maybe we can use that to our advantage." Daniel said, as he looked toward the creature.

"How can we use that. He's out there, we are in here. He's not going to let us out." Jen insisted.

"Maybe he would, if you make nice." Malachi said, as he nodded towards the doorway.

"No! I am not going anywhere near that thing. No way!" She insisted.

"Jen, we are not suggesting you do anything, but get his attention. Maybe, get him to open the energy doorway. Then we take care of him." Daniel tried to reassure her.

"Are you going to hurt him?" She asked

"No, but if he is unconscious, his hold on our powers will release."

"Understood. I just don't know what to do."

"Just be nice to him." Malachi said, pushing her to the doorway.

Jen walked forward, studying the dark-skinned creature. She looked him up and down, doing her best to smile at him. As the creature watched her, it turned its head and looked back. Jen reached the edge of the doorway, as the creature began to move closer to her.

Jen's stomach began to turn, as she forced herself to stand so close to him. Her mind flashed to the day the dark water abomination tried to kill her. She tried hard to push her feelings down. She wondered if it could sense her fear.

"Hello, do you remember me?" Jen asked.

The creature moved its head in a motion to acknowledge her.

"I remember you." She smiled at him. "You like me, don't you?"

The creature smiled back, unaware of her intention, and unable to speak.

"I'd like to know you better, but I am trapped inside here. I know Raven said we had to be here, but you could allow me to come out and talk to you." Jen said, as she tried to gain his sympathy.

The creature moved his mouth and moaned, as if he was speaking. It was obvious, he was scared of Raven. He appeared to be very simple minded. As Jen watched him, she was sure he was not much more than a child mentally. She turned back to look at Daniel. She did not want to hurt the creature; he was simply being manipulated by Raven.

Daniel shook his head at Jen, he also saw what she did. Jen turned back to the creature and tried to sooth him as she asked him to open the doorway for her to come out. The creature came close to her and looked into her eyes. He was willing to do as she asked.

As she stepped out into the open, the creature stood, staring at her. Daniel and Malachi moved around behind him. Daniel raised a rock and prepared to hit the creature from behind.

"No! Daniel don't do it. I don't want you to hurt him. We'll find another way." Jen insisted.

Before Jen could finish her sentence, Malachi slammed a rock into the back of the creature's head.

It fell to the floor as Jen watched. She fell to her knees, and looked at the dark black blood, that oozed from the tear in its skin.

"Why the hell did you do that? We could have escaped." Jen screamed.

"Not without the ability to orb." Malachi insisted. "And what if they come for us."

"You did not know they would."

"Oh, I think he is right." Raven called out. "You aren't going anywhere."

Chapter Eleven: The Darkness Within

Jen raised her eyes, to see her fears realized. The demons had returned. She turned to Daniel, and then to the dark water creature, still lying on the floor. Then she realized Malachi was right, for all the wrong reasons.

Jen still pitied the creature, but she knew what had to be done. She closed her eyes for a second, as the power within her grew. As she opened her eyes, they glowed a bright white light. Soon, Daniel joined her, as they began to focus their power.

"You know Raven, I think you are wrong. We will be leaving." Jen spoke with confidence.

"What can you do? You have no power here." Raven spoke with a false sense of superiority.

Raven started to turn, as she was sure Jen was wrong. She thought it better the demons take the brunt of their force, rather than her. She did not make it but a few steps, when the force of their power tore through the underworld.

Their combined energy mingled, and turned a bright bluish tint, as it disintegrated everything in its path. As the demons ran, their skin burst into flames, melting, falling downwards into smoldering masses. And then there was Raven, who hid behind a shield, created from the power she drew from the demons before they fell.

Malachi walked forward to her, "How long do you think that wall will hold?"

"You are such a stupid fool. We could have been together. The two of us could have ruled the underworld." The words spewed from her mouth, as she spit at him.

"You and I, could never have been anything." He spoke, as he studied her shield. "I am not a demon. I may be an Angel of Death, but I am so much more. More than you deserve."

As Malachi turned from her, he felt the darkness within him. It wanted to claim her in death. He fought himself to retain his humanity. It was a powerful struggle, but in light of what he recently learned, he knew he had more to fight for.

As he returned to Daniel's side, he looked up, and his eyes turned dark black. Daniel stepped back, uncertain of what was happening. He took ahold of Jen, and moved her behind him. As she stepped back, Jen peaked around Daniel's shoulder, to see a sight that made her skin crawl.

Malachi turned back towards Raven. His humanity was overcome by the dark energy. It wanted revenge on her. Nothing short of her death, would satisfy the darkness. He spread his hands, and formed an all too familiar dark energy crossbow. This time it was different. The darkness drew upon his angel heritage, and used the power he never knew he had.

The arrow formed within the crossbow. Where it had once only been black and glowing, now it took on a bright flame. Malachi looked down and smiled at his creation. He was not totally aware of what he was doing. The dark energy washed over him, controlling his every move. Still, he honestly believed he was in control.

Like a puppet, he aimed the crossbow at Raven. There was no conscious reasoning of right or wrong, when he sent the arrow soaring towards her. Raven gasped, as she knew what was about to happen. She scrambled to raise her powers, as the arrow struck, shattering her shield.

Raven faded from view, as the arrow pierced her skin. The shield may have slowed its approach, but the flaming point found its mark. With her, she took the dark water creature. Malachi looked on, as his dark crossbow disappeared.

He stood there in confusion, as he hung his head. His breathing increased, sending him into a state that looked as if he were hyperventilating. He turned back to Daniel, to ask why.

"What have I done?" He asked in a shaky voice.

"I'm not really sure, but I believe the power used your body, to do its will." Daniel said, shrugging his shoulders.

"I didn't even know. I had no control." Malachi said swallowing hard. "I want this out of me…now."

Chapter Twelve: Dark Versus Light

Jen looked down where the dark water creature had been. Nothing was left, but the dark pool of blood on the floor. "I guess he will go on being a pawn for her use. Funny, but I feel bad for him, even though he once tried to cause my death. Maybe, I am starting to lose it."

"Nope, you are just as human as the rest of us." Daniel said laughing, realizing none of them were quite human anymore.

"We need to get out of here." Jen said looking around her. "Elizabeth, are you still there?"

In an open space of the chamber, Elizabeth appeared in a shaft of light. As she stepped forward, she looked around. The sight of the place, both scared and disgusted her. She was almost sure where they were.

"Where the hell have you brought me?" She asked.

"The Underworld." Daniel opened his mouth, almost waiting for the lecture.

"I know that look. Something bad happened. Don't worry, we will skip the speech for now." She said smiling at him. "But you, Jen, know better."

"Wasn't my idea. I was just an innocent bystander, who got dragged into this." Jen defended herself.

"I seem to remember you sneaking away to join the party."

"Can't blame a girl for trying." Jen said laughing.

"We need to get out of here before any demons show up." Elizabeth spoke, with an urgency in her voice.

"Demons showed, captured and we took them out." Malachi added.

"How bad is this?" Elizabeth asked.

"Several demons, Raven and a dark water creature bad." Jen said shaking her head. "And, Malachi was taken over by the darkness in his veins."

"I feared this, the darkness is gaining strength. Ok, let's get out of here, and deal with the rest in a safer environment. Everyone join hands, I am taking us above ground."

Elizabeth extended her light over them all, as she took them into her orb. Above ground, they materialized inside the chapel of the cemetery, which they all knew too well. As the light disappeared, Jen made her way to a bench, and sat down.

"Are you OK?" Daniel asked.

"Yeah, just my stomach is queasy. This is all still kinda new to me. I'll be alright. No time to be sick now."

"You will get it in time sweetheart. Group orbs are a bit disorienting." Elizabeth spoke, as she put a hand on Jen's shoulder. "Now for you Malachi, I think I know what happened to you down there.

The place is filled with dark energy and evil. Your darkness, fed off of it."

"Maybe, but how did I keep it in check when Muerte had me below?" He asked.

"You were in her catacombs, she shielded them with a balance of good and evil. Just like her own existence, she was neither one or the other. Just an Angel of Death. Which concerns me."

"Why? Is something wrong?" Jen asked.

"Yes, there is no Angel of Death now. No one is collecting the dead. Throughout the timeline, the dead are piling up." As she spoke, her voice sounded stressed.

"What can we do?" Malachi asked.

"I would be tempted, to send you into the timeline, to do Muerte's work, but I feel that would be a mistake."

"Why…can't he do some of the work, while we straighten out this mess?" Jen tried to make sense of it all.

"Like it or not, Malachi should never have become an Angel of Death. He has another destiny, one which he would have fulfilled, if not for his father's interference." Elizabeth explained.

"Then, how do we straighten this out?" Malachi asked.

"I feel the whole thing is about to straighten itself out."

"Do you know something we do not?" Daniel asked.

"Yes…And there is nothing I can do about it, except let it play out on its own." Elizabeth turned away, not wanting to reveal her hand. She knew something big was coming, and she had no power over it.

Chapter Thirteen: The Dead Will Rise

In a chapel in the cemetery, the four stayed, unaware of what was coming. Jen looked around the walls, studying the familiar place. It had not changed since she lost Daniel, that night when the light came for him. She shivered a bit, when she remembered how she thought she had lost him.

It was not all that long ago, but so much had happened since then. She had lost her family, died at the hands of a demon and then returned to be a Whitelighter. Nothing was simple or innocent anymore. Jen put her head down for a moment on the bench, and drifted in a waking dream of that night.

~~~~~~
~~~~~~

They arrived at the old chapel just as night fell. Jen could actually see the stars from time to time. It was the first night that the rain had not been pelting down. She enjoyed the quiet. The clouds outside were moving in and out. In between clouds, the light from the moon would shine through the stained-glass windows and warm the room with its glow. The whole room reminded her of a rainbow. Jen looked around and smiled.

"This is nice." She spoke.

"Yeah, I'm glad we are here."

"Look, just in case something happens, I just wanted to say thank-you."

"For what?" Daniel asked."

"For a lot of things, but mostly for showing me that it is Ok to be happy. I haven't been this happy in a long time. It's all because of you."

"I feel the same way. I never fell in love when I was alive, I'm glad if it had to happen in death, that it was with you."

Just as Daniel finished his words, the light started in the doorway. The door flew open, and the swirls of light caused a wind to gush through the place. It was different than before. The wind was forceful and gusting. It felt like a storm had entered the room. As the wind blew, paintings ripped from the wall. As Jen ran to take Daniel's hand, one of the paintings struck her in the forehead, knocking her unconscious.

Daniel turned to help Jen. When he realized she was out cold, he pulled her up onto a pew and tried to get her out of the way of the debris. Then he turned to the light. "So, you want me.... you better know I am not going down without a fight." With that said, Daniel tapped into all the energy he had, and generated a shield around himself, just as he had done to protect Jen.

The winds beat in his direction, pummeling him, in an attempt to weaken the shield. The light from the vortex grew brighter. With every second, it encompassed the room. Daniel knew he could not keep this up forever. He fought long and hard, with every bit of energy he had. Until the light broke through his shield. Just as his light started to flicker, Jen regained consciousness.

She sat up and saw what was happening. Jen realized she had been unconscious for a long time. "I won't let you take him," she screamed, running in the path of the light.   "Jen no!" Daniel screamed back, just as the light engulfed her.

Inside the light, there was no strong wind. Just like the eye of a hurricane, it was calm and everything was peaceful. 'Why is it this way?' Jen wondered. And then a familiar face appeared to her. Just like before, the image appeared and took form. It was her grandmother. She was there in the light with Jen.

"Jen, my darling girl, you have to leave. You don't belong here."

"No, I won't let them take Daniel."

"The light comes for those when it is there time. And now is not your time dear."

"Grandma, I can't let him go, I love him."

"I know you do, but you cannot forfeit your life to save his."

"What else can I do?"

"Go back my dear, and live your life. You dying here, will change nothing."

"There has to be a way." Jen pleaded.

"There is nothing humanly possible that you can do."

"Wait, if it is not humanly possible, is it possible for a spirit?"

"Perhaps, tell Daniel to fight the shadows. He will understand. But I have told you too much. For now, you have to go." And with one swipe of her grandmother's hand, Jen went flying out of the light, and back to Daniel's side.

She turned to Daniel, "You can beat it, Grandma said you have to fight the shadows. She said you would know when it happened." Daniel smiled at her and took her hand, "You have to go now. I have to do this alone." And he pushed her out of the way, and walked towards the light. He decided that fighting it all night would wear him down, and if he was going to have to fight, then it was time.

The light was too bright for Jen to see anymore. Daniel was inside of it, and it encompassed him. She wished there was something she could do. But there was not. The light began to pulse and change in form. The wind that had filled the chapel, died down. Jen heard the crackle of static electricity sounding through the place. And in an instant, the light was gone. No light, and no Daniel.

She hung her head and cried. Even though she knew it would happen, she still wasn't prepared. There was nothing she could do. She sat on the floor of the chapel and pulled her knees up to her chest.

~~~~~~

Jen awoke from her dream, as a storm began to slam against the outer walls of the cemetery. It was so familiar to her. The storm came in fast and
~~~~~~

felt paranormal in nature. She moved towards the door, and touched the handle. As she did, her mind was flooded with images of the dead.

Jen stepped back bumping into Daniel, who had come up behind her. She turned, trying to catch her breath. She was scared and Daniel knew it. Jen wasn't one to give into her fear, but this time she was frightened. The images, were too much like when she died in the lake, as all the dead bodies surrounded her and dragged her to the bottom.

"What is it? What did you see?" He asked.

"The dead are coming, and I do not mean a few. There is an army forming. They know Muerte is no longer here to claim them. Daniel, we can't stop them. There will be too many"

Chapter Fourteen: An Angel Of Death Returns

Jen walked to the window and looked out over the cemetery. It was dark and gloomy. The only thing that helped her to see, were the blasts of lightning that illuminated from the sky to the ground. She watched intently as she counted in her head the time between the rolls of thunder. She thought about it, and it seemed like a childish thing to do in counting. It did let her know that the storm was getting closer.

As she watched, she studied the tombstones, at least the ones she could see clearly. There was no sign of the dead yet, but she feared it was only a matter of time before they saw signs of them. Daniel walked up behind her, and put his arms around her waist.

"Don't worry, we will survive this, just like we have survived so many other things." Daniel tried to reassure her. "Just remember, we have an army of angels on our side. Good and evil are in balance. No one is going to let an army of dead people mess with that."

"I hear what you are saying, and I want to believe it. Maybe I am just scared of what happened when the dead drug me down into the water." Jen shivered, as the image of the skeletons and decaying bodies reached out for her.

~~~~~~

As the demon Abraxas, known to others as the Black Hat Man, looked down at the two girls running to hide behind a mausoleum, he called out to Malachi. A dark cloud appeared, as the Darklighter shimmered into view. The demon pointed to the two unknowing victims. Malachi looked to him and smiled. He already knew what needed to be done.
~~~~~~

"Take care of our two little trespassers. I don't like unwanted spectators." The Black Hat Man said laughing.

"No problem. I scattered the one girl's spirit before. As for the human, I love target practice." Malachi spoke, with a sinister sound in his voice.

"No, I have other plans for her. Just get her moving in the direction of the flood. Let's see if she can swim."

Malachi moved in closer, until he was just behind the girls. As they prepared to run, he pulled his hands apart and formed his black energy bow. Pulling on the string, an arrow formed. He aimed for Abigail. As he turned loose the string, he smiled and spoke. "Good-bye again."

Jen was ahead of Abigail, and never saw the arrow coming. As Abigail fell to the ground, she turned loose of Jen's hand. Jen stopped and spun around, to see Abigail fall. The arrow had hit its mark, and Jen watched as the black energy coated her friend's body. The life force that was Abigail's faded, as Jen pulled her close.

"No, Abigail, please, don't go." Jen screamed as rain washed over her face.

"It's too late. I have been here before. Except this time, I think it is the last. Take care of yourself and Daniel. Be happy my sister." Her voice faded to a whisper, as Abigail's life force ended.

Jen screamed, as the energy the held Abigail's form dissolved, until there was nothing left. Jen became frantic. She had to get to Daniel. As she ran for the open area to try to spot him, the Black Hat Man watched her. "And now my dear, it is your turn. I said I would have you. And now I will."

As the demon walked towards Jen, he commanded the water flow to increase from the bottom of the overflowing lake. As Jen ran, the water flowed faster in her direction, and she was unaware, until she saw the wall approaching. It was too late to get away. The water hit her hard, and lifted her from the ground and flipped her limp body into the lower flooded area.

Jen struggled to get above the water, as it swirled about her. She couldn't breathe. She tried to scream for help, but her mouth only filled with the muddy dirt-filled water. She managed to get above, and spit up what she had taken in. She tried to scream, but no one heard her. Taking a deep breath, she swam as hard as she could.

The Black Hat Man watched her in amusement. "Perhaps I made it too easy for you." He spit forth, as he drove more water down the hill. With the wave, came caskets and tombstones, which were ripped up and beat against each other breaking them into small projectiles.

As Jen struggled to stay above water, the next wave hit her and she drifted underneath. The pieces of tombstones flew into the water all around her, like bullets from a high-powered rifle. One piece hit Jen's shoulder, ripping the flesh open to a point that she had to stop and hold tight to it. As she looked away, she did not see the coffins, flying down the hillside in the waters flow. As they flew into the flooded area, their lids came open, and the dead were scattered in the water all around her.

Jen turned to scream, as she saw the rotted corpses. She struggled to get away, as they moved closer. Like animated puppets, they reached out and grabbed ahold of her. They held tight, and prevented Jen from swimming, as she sank deeper. Jen let out one last fatal scream, as they drug her into the deep water.

The Black Hat Man stood just out of the way. "I told you I would have you. I never lie." He laughed, as he turned his attention back to the battle. Jen's life was over, as she disappeared from the water, in a bright ball of light.

~~~~~~

Jen caught herself, sinking into the disgust created from her flashback. She tried to fight it off,
~~~~~~

and told herself, she was still there with Daniel. Maybe in a way, she was better, now she was more than human and had all these abilities. The more she reasoned, the less it comforted her.

As Jen turned, her eyes locked onto Malachi. She tried to tell herself, that the person from her memory, had been under the control of the darkness within him. Still, she did not trust him. He was too quick to kill or harm others. If he were truly an angel underneath, then why was he not fighting the darkness. He was ready to take out the dark water creature with no remorse. She stood there just staring at him, wondering if there was any good in him at all. She realized he had become the Angel of Death Muerte wanted him to be.

Chapter Fifteen: From The Dead Of Night

Malachi felt as if he was being watched. His paranoia was taking over. Then he turned his head slightly and saw Jen. The way she looked at him, drove a shiver through his spine. He was worried, maybe she had not forgiven the past. In her current form, she was capable of winning in any competition against him. He shook his head; they were not against each other, and he had to stop thinking like that.

Jen turned back to the window. As she looked out over the grounds, she watched, not knowing what she expected to find. Then out of the darkness, she saw a figure. It came slowly between the mausoleums. She was sure it was there, but each time she looked to get a better glimpse, it disappeared.

"You guys, there is something out there. It is moving about, and I can't quite make out what it is, Still, I know I saw it."

As Elizabeth came to the window, and scanned the area. "Are you sure it wasn't just your eyes playing tricks on you?" She asked.

"No, I saw it. In the flashes of light, you can make out the form clearly. It just keeps appearing and disappearing."

As they hovered by the window, the bursts of lightning came. With each one, they stared waiting for something. Then nothing, each time. As they were about to give up, the last bolt of lightning was bright and lit the whole area.

"There it is! Jen was right." Daniel yelled out excitedly.

"Told you." Jen said with confidence. "But what is it. That can't be human."

Elizabeth scanned the area, as she opened her mouth. "No, that is most certainly not human. We need to know what it is, and why it is here. One of us needs to do some surveillance."

"I'll do it." Daniel spoke, trying to muster his courage.

As Daniel went to the door of the chapel, he looked out, and made sure he was not seen. He walked down the steps, and over to the asphalt road, which cut through the center of the area.

As he walked, he constantly scanned, to see if anyone was lurking. He did not want to be taken by surprise, by the dead or any other creature. He studied the grounds, as he turned the corner near where the creature had been.

Something was strange about the cemetery. There were no ghosts. He thought back to the time of Abraxas, and how he had collected the spirits of the dead, to draw on their power, but surely there would have been ghosts who returned to the grounds. There had to be new ghosts arriving. When he first came to the cemetery sixty years earlier, he remembered the ghosts arrived daily. The ones who had no place to go, and clung to their bodies. There were even the ones who came there for asylum.

Something about all this was wrong, and Daniel sensed it. His abilities had grown, and become more powerful, since he took on the role of a Whitelighter. He had recently developed the ability to sense things. He had no control over it, but it seemed to be getting stronger.

Something about what he was sensing was familiar. As if he was tuning into a person he had known. It did not make sense to him. No one he knew, would be in the cemetery. Still, he could not shake the feeling.

"I see you have come back." A voice called out to him.

"What? Who said that?" Daniel called back, fearful of who he might find.

"It's me, Hershal. I remember you, back when you were a spirit trapped here. That seems to have changed. You look almost human now. The prophecy, was true I assume.”

“You are still here. I thought all the ghosts had gone. I haven’t seen one besides you.” Daniel replied.

“Yeah, they are hiding. They know something is coming. They don’t want to be a part of it.” Hershal spoke with a roughness to his voice. “I just don’t have time for such foolishness. I have been here for more decades than I can count. I am not going to run at the drop of a hat.

Hershal looked up to Daniel, and laughed out loud. He was quite a site, with his old military outfit. He had been in the cemetery waiting for something special to happen, but it never did. His only calling was to sit by his stone, and watch as the others came and went. The light never came for him, but then, it did not come for everyone. He was no more special than anyone else.

“You are quite a funny old man you know.” Daniel said laughing.

"Watch it young man. I might be a ghost, but I can take offense."

Daniel wiped away the steady stream of rain that poured over his face and eyes. "I meant no insult. I happen to like you very much. I think we should all have as much spunk as you. Look, I am searching for a figure, we saw from the chapel. It was tall and thin, wearing some sort of robes. It came through here just minutes ago. Did you happen to see it?"

"I see everything that happens here. I also know when to keep my mouth shut. What came through here is dangerous. I have seen that one before. A soul collector. I don't want no part of it."

"What do you mean soul collector?" Daniel asked.

"It's one of those, who come to take the dead, whether they are willing or not. There is darkness there. Very dangerous." Hershal was terrified, and Daniel could see it.

"I understand your point. I will be careful."

"No, it you go messing with things you aren't supposed to, you will be worse than dead. You will be destroyed."

Daniel looked at Hershal, trying to be respectful of his oddity. "Thank you, Hershal. I will be going now. Stay safe."

"Daniel. What happened to the girl you came with before? I heard bad things. I didn't want to believe them. I really liked her, she was special."

"She's OK, and up in the chapel right now. Maybe after all this is done, I will bring her by to visit you."

"I'd like that. You know, old ghosts like me, don't get many visitors. Especially pretty ones that we like."

Daniel looked up and smiled at him. "I'll be sure she comes by, as soon as she can. Good-bye."

As Daniel walked down the road, leading towards the center of the cemetery, he saw the shadow passing by the back of a mausoleum. He moved quickly and came up behind the dark creature.

He stopped short to look at it, before calling out to tell it to stop.

As the creature spun around, he swore he knew it. A woman, he thought. Then she spread her arms, and blasted him with a blinding light. By the time his eyes cleared, she was gone. All he was sure of; was he knew this woman.

Chapter Sixteen: She Walks In Darkness

Daniel orbed back to the chapel, appearing inside the door. As he stepped out of the bright blue light, a wave of water came with him. He was soaked from head to toe, from the increasing storm. Standing there, he shook off as much water as he could. He felt as if he had brought the storm indoors, with the amount of water he left on the floor.

"Did you see anything?" Elizabeth said moving closer to him.

"Yes, I saw the figure. It was a woman. One, I assume, did not want to be seen, because she temporarily blinded me with light." He explained.

"Have you ever seen her before?" Malachi's voice was shaky. He feared the idea of this woman, but did not know why.

"My senses, tell me I knew her. She was so familiar, but not in appearance, I did not have a clue." Daniel was confused. "Maybe she was a shape shifter or was wearing a disguise. I don't know. All I do know; is she did not want to permanently hurt me."

"At least you are alright." Jen said stopping short of hugging him. "Wow, you are really wet."

"I know. As I was walking, I kept scanning for ghosts. There were none. The only one I found in the end was Hershal."

"You mean that funny old military ghost. I loved him," Jen said smiling.

"Yeah, well the feeling is mutual. I promised him, I would bring you back for a visit."

"Aww, if we survive the attack of the dead, that will be nice." Jen said sarcastically.

Elizabeth shot Jen an unapproving look, before walking back to the window. She watched as the cemetery seemed to change. There were shadowy figures, rising upwards from the ground. She focused in trying to see what they were. The heavy rain, disguised their movements, but she was sure of what she saw. The dead had begun to rise.

"It's starting. I'm heading upstairs to gather reinforcements. We are going to need as much help as we can get with this." Elizabeth said, before disappearing in a shaft of light.

Malachi made his way to the window, and watched, as his heart beat louder in his chest. He was an Angel of Death, but all of a sudden, he feared the dead. He turned away and tried to muster his courage.

Jen watched, as Malachi sat down on the back bench. She studied him. Her powers as an empath, had never worked as far as he was concerned. She was scared to try now, since he was changing. Then again, she wondered why she cared. He did after all, have a hand in her death. She just kept reminding herself, he was an innocent and the darkness had control. It was as if he were two people in the same body. His inner angel had to be set free, and the dark one removed.

Jen moved to his side. She did not open her mouth, for fear of saying the wrong thing. She wanted to find peace with the hatred she felt inside for him. Perhaps, if she saved him, it would make a difference.

"I never meant to hurt you." He began to speak. I look back and remember. It seems like I was on the inside, looking out, as someone else pulled the strings.

"I am trying to come to terms with what happened. I know what you are saying is true, and for that, I do not kill you." Jen laughed.

"I wouldn't blame you if you did."

"Nope, I am an angel now…for lack of better term, a Whitelighter. I fight for good and the innocent. And in a way, you are an innocent. Even though you asked for what Muerte did to you, it was for the good of another. You wanted to save your Uncle, and for that, I will attempt to help you."

"Thank you, I do not know what else to say," Malachi turned to smile at her. His eyes clear of the darkness for the moment.

"Then you will understand why I have to do this." Jen reached over and grabbed tight to his hand, as she used her powers as an empath to penetrate his brain.

Images flew at her hard and fast, as she scanned his past, and attempted to see images of his future. They flashed back, on his change to a Darklighter, and the power bestowed on him, as an Angel of Death. She felt his pain, and the fear he lived with. Then the confusion, of the returned memories his father had taken, then given back. Then there was the darkness.

It was aware of her presence, there in his mind. It watched her with amusement. She was no threat to it. She had no power over this creature the darkness possessed. Still, it watched, and waited for her to venture too far into its territory.

And then she went too far, as she witnessed his future. The woman of immense power. She was coming. She would change everything. Malachi would bow down to her. The darkness would make sure of that. Then, Jen turned to leave. She knew she was being watched.

"Leaving so soon, child of light." The demonic voice, echoed all through her head.

"Yeah, I have what I need." Jen replied.

"A warning for the future. Stay out of the way of darkness. It took your life once. Maybe, it could happen again, if you get in our way."

"You don't scare me. I have faced high powered demons, and yes, even death…and I am still here. Back off, I am leaving." Jen let go of Malachi, as she came out of her trance.

"Is everything alright." Malachi asked.

"Yes, everything is fine." Jen smiled, as she lied to him.

Chapter Seventeen: A Light In The Darkness

A bright light rose from the cemetery. Inside, a lone angel seeking protection and support. Elizabeth's mind raced as she climbed upwards. Her only thought was, that she did not have time for this foolishness. It seemed all she did in recent years, was save the world of the living, from this crisis or that. She grew weary of always being on the front line.

She materialized in the Upper Realm, just inside the guardians watch station. It was no secret, they already knew of the situation, with the way they were running back and forth. Each guardian had their own observation window. All, to different places and times. All, working together to keep a balance in time and places.

Elizabeth walked over to number 15. He was in charge of the area she had just left. He was scanning the area and shaking his head. He just kept moaning the words, "Not Right." She did not want to disturb him, but she needed help.

"I know you are busy, but what is happening?" She asked.

"I would say, all hell is breaking loose." He responded.

"I know, the dead have risen. I was there, and have firsthand experience." She said quickly. "But why?"

"Simple, the dead are rising, because no one is there to keep them in check. Muerte is gone, now they are running free."

"Yes, I agree, but how are they doing it on their own. They need a power to initiate this." Elizabeth insisted.

"They do have one. It is demonic in nature." He added. "It started months ago, with Abraxas."

"Yes, but he is dead. I was there, I watched him be disintegrated."

"Yes, but power does not just go away. Sometimes it takes another form." He said, as he pointed to the view screen and replayed the night of Abraxas' death."

Elizabeth watched, as the scene played out. Jen came for the demon. He underestimated her, believing she was still human. He learned the hard way, that she had become an angel. Then she lifted him into the air, and destroyed him at a molecular level.

"Ok, that is what I saw. So, how did he survive?" She asked.

"Watch…now pay attention to the spray of power leaving his body. Now, look behind the mausoleum, to the left. It is…."

"Malachi." She said, finishing his line. "But…how?"

"Raven. That is how he obtained the power, and also why she has been running after him the whole time. She knew she could not channel such power into herself, but a powerful receptor like Malachi was perfect. She just wants him so she can use the power for her own goals." Number 15 was proud of himself for solving the mystery.

"Malachi has been acting strange and battling his darkness for control. Is it possible Abraxas is inside of him?"

"Not only possible, but probable. He is trying to take over, I would say. All that power and inside a young strong body. I would bet money on it." Number 15 said, as he drew her attention to the screen. "The dead in the cemetery, are making their way towards the chapel. They will need your help."

"Yes, about that, if it is Abraxas, how is he controlling the dead. He could only deal with spirits who were willing?"

"There is someone else at play here. I will continue to look into it. For now, get back to the young ones." He insisted.

Elizabeth orbed herself to an area just beyond the chapel. She watched as the dead marched forward. The crowd was filled with the recently dead, their grey skin, coated in the rainfall. With them, were the remains of those who had died decades before, and others who hardly had remains at all.

As the thunder rolled in, it sounded like an army going to war. The blasts of lightning, illuminated their zombie like features. Elizabeth felt a shiver, as she looked at the remains of the once living.

The whole thing puzzled her. If Abraxas left enough power behind to raise them, then who was directing them. It could not be coming from Malachi; he was holding onto his control. There had to be another.

Chapter Eighteen: Return Of The Dead

Elizabeth stepped out into the road, and walked behind the army, that advanced towards her friends. She contemplated what to do. A wave of her energy could possibly wipe them all out, but that would do nothing for the others worldwide that all had their own agendas.

She studied them as they moved like mindless automatons. They were little more than puppets. This army of the dead, did not possess intelligence. She knew Abraxas had been powerful, but did he have it within himself to control so many lifeless creatures at once. Only an Angel of Death possessed that much power, she thought to herself.

And then, it came to her. If someone else was accessing Malachi and the power of darkness he had within, they could accomplish this. There were no other Angels of Death. There was only one at a time, replaced at the time the older would die.

Then it dawned on her, if the dead rose, maybe an Angel Of Death rose with them. Someone started this, then it was handed off to another. One who was more deadly than all of them put together.

Elizabeth studied the army as it moved along. She was looking for that one figure. She knew it had to be there. Quickly, she ran behind the force until she saw it. There she was, Elizabeth was sure, but she could not take this on alone.

As she orbed inside the chapel, she found the others watching outside. They turned to her, having seen her light return to the cemetery. Moving closer to her, they were eager to hear what she had learned.

"We have to get out of here. The army is moving this way and will be at the door in minutes."

"Who is behind this? Daniel asked.

"That is the weird part. It is Abraxas." Elizabeth answered.

"How is that possible? I killed him. I saw him die." Jen said, in a confused state.

"Yes, you did. But he did not die entirely. His power just changed states and was directed into a new host." She said, pointing towards Malachi."

"Why are you pointing at me? I don't understand."

"When Abraxas disintegrated, Raven channeled his energy into you, since she could not handle it in her weak body." Elizabeth explained.

"Is that why, all of a sudden, I am fighting to control my own body?" He asked.

"Yes, and the power you possess, was used to raise the dead. It was like someone knew how to use your own abilities, mixed with Abraxas, to initiate a process."

"A process, someone else is controlling." Daniel added.

"Yes, and I would say it is an Angel of Death." Malachi added.

"Yeah, but I thought there was only one at a time. Oh boy, you are not trying to say she is back in dead form?" Jen lowered her eyes at the thought of it.

"How can we fight her? When she was just normal, we had little control. Now as a creature with her own power, and that of Abraxas to draw on. How can we win?" Malachi said, feeling the darkness inside him churning. He felt like a victim. Not only had he been changed and stripped of his humanity once, now a demon was inside him, adding to the process. "I don't care what it takes, I want this out of me."

"We will find a way. We just need to be careful and make sure the process is done right. Or something could…." Daniel's words trailed off.

"You mean, it will fight on the way out, and I might die…that's what you are saying. Right!" Malachi was angry…. angrier than he had ever been.

"Stop!" Elizabeth shouted. "We don't have time for this. The dead are at the door. We have to get out of here. We will deal with the darkness soon. For now, we have to get past them, and to the cause of this problem."

Each making their own way, they left the chapel, and reappeared out onto the street. Daniel searched the crowd and found his target. He looked to the others, and turned back to orb.

Deep inside the line of dead, she stood. Looking like a statue, that had once been a woman. Her hands, that reached out from her robe, were withered, like skin stretched on decaying bone. Her face had once had features, now they sank into her skull, and revealed the lines, that ran around her eyes and nose. Her skin was so thin, you could see the teeth that hid behind her dark colored lips.

She stood there and allowed the rain that poured down, to wash over her exposed body. She wished it would penetrate and fill her from within. But she knew it could not. Only water that was offered as a gift to her, could be absorbed. Until the next gift, she would stay the shriveled state she was.

Daniel had heard the stories, of how the creature traveled through time and place, to answer the prayers of the dying. Many did not know if she was good or evil. She had become a religious figure, because of her title Angel of Death. Daniel hoped there was some good left in her, or at least a way to reach the good.

He moved towards her, and before she noticed him, Daniel laid a hand on her shoulder and pulled her into his orb. The bright blue light he emitted, filled the dark street of the cemetery, as he bounced backwards to the trees behind them. With the woman out of reach for a moment, the army stopped and stood in place like the lifeless remains they were.

As the others came forward, they saw the creature before them. She stood quietly observing her situation. Then she pulled back her hood to show her face. Malachi drew back in fear and disbelief. His only word to leave his mouth, "Muerte."

"You did not think I could be destroyed so easily did you. I am all powerful. I am universal. Your sad attempt to destroy me was humorous. I have returned stronger than you would have ever known me to be. Now joined with the power of Abraxas, I will be superior to everyone." As she spoke, her words echoed through the cemetery, and her army of the dead began to move again. Her laughter filled the air as the corpses moved towards her.

Chapter Nineteen: The Mistress Of The Darkness

The army came forward and encircled them. Malachi trembled at the thought of his fate. He had to find a way out of this. He could not let the others be destroyed by his mistakes. Looking at Muerte, he remembered how he summoned her. If she was reverted back to her old state, then maybe he could win her back with a simple gift.

He looked around. He needed a bowl or something to collect water in. Beside him on a tombstone, was a simple stone chalice. He grabbed it, and pulled it from the display of flowers left there. It had some water in it, which he used to clean it out, then he held it up, as the heavy rain began to fill it.

"What the hell are you doing?" Jen asked.

"Hopefully, getting ready to save our lives. Just give me a minute, and pray this works."

He held the chalice high in the air, as the rain quickly filled it. Then turning towards Muerte, he held the water out to her. She looked down and recognized his gesture. She bowed her head, and looked into the water.

"You summoned me like this once before. I want to remember it, but my memories are clouded. My past is still a part of me, just somewhere I cannot get to." Muerte spoke in her haggard voice."

"Here…take the water, this gift may help you find your way back to who you were." Malachi encouraged her.

Muerte took hold of the chalice, and raised it to her dried lips. She took in a little, and then let the remaining water absorb into her skin. She basked in the joyful feeling of hydration. She no longer felt like a dried-out husk. As the moisture moved throughout her body, her features changed, and she once again saw her skin revert to more like a human.

"Do you remember now?" Malachi asked.

"Yes, I do. I remember you." She smiled at him. "You tried to kill me, to escape our contract."

As she continued to smile, she reached out a now flesh covered hand, and took ahold of his throat. Malachi tried to scream out, as she cut off his ability to breathe. Muerte lifted him from the ground, as she attempted to take the life from him.

"Stop!" Daniel screamed out.

"And why should I?"

"He is not totally to blame for his actions. When Abraxas died, his power was placed in Malachi, and mixed with the darkness you added to him. He never knew it was there. It took him over at times, and made him an unwilling victim." Daniel tried to explain.

Muerte held Malachi in the air, as she studied him, and tried to decide if it was the truth. She lowered him slightly and looked into his eyes. She knew the look of darkness that was placed there. It had changed. She could tell just by the look of him.

"This was done by a demon. Not a powerful one." She said, as she studied him.

"Yes, it was Raven. She was looking for a way to gain power, as usual." Elizabeth spoke.

"She should be punished for this." Muerte said, making a face of disgust.

"I have battled her before, but she just keeps coming back." Elizabeth said sarcastically.

"Maybe this time, I will help you?"

"I would welcome that." Elizabeth said smiling. She remembered all too well their last battle.

~~~~~~

"I was wondering when I would bump into you." Elizabeth's voice echoed through the barn as she took full form.

"I was just admiring Daniel's handy work. There might be hope for him yet."
~~~~~~

"Hope? And what hope would you be thinking of?"

Raven laughed out loud wickedly, "Hope that he will turn to the side of evil. You know, he does have the right to choose. That is if he survives those pesky Shadow People. They can be such a pain in the ass, but I don't have to tell you that, do I?"

"And what makes you even imagine you could make this boy evil?"

"He has already killed. The first Shadow died by means of the truck, and we'll call that one a pass for Daniel. But this one died by his own hands."

"The boy is pure, and his light is brighter than most I have seen. He won't turn. And as for this mess, he defended his life. He has not learned the intricacies of fighting with his new powers…but he will." Elizabeth mocked her.

"And of course, mommy Elizabeth will be there to claim him for the side of good."

"Oh, poor Raven. You still hate me, after all this time, don't you?" Elizabeth teased her.

"I couldn't give a rat's ass about you. My, are we feeling self-important?"

"No, I just know you have turned this into some kind of competition. Since the day I cast you out, you have gone out of your way to convert my Charges."

"Can't blame me for trying, can you? I'm not really so bad you know, just a perfectionist."

"You know there has to be a balance between good and evil. Neither can exist without the other." Elizabeth stared her in the eyes.

"I beg to differ with you. I think evil might just do a good job, if we were in charge for a while." Raven insisted.

"The Elders will never let that happen. They will destroy you, before they let the likes of a low-level demon be in charge of anything."

"All this, because I want your newest charge, that is so funny. What are you scared of Elizabeth? Things not going as well as the forces of good want?"

"I won't even go there with you. The world is in balance and you know it."

"For the moment, you are right, but things do change. Just like Daniel may change. We know how powerful he is. We have been watching. He is a chosen one. You people hide in your white light and think you can keep secrets like this. He has the ability to be a god and you know it." Raven screamed in hatred.

"Daniel is special; no one said he was not. And because of that, I am watching over him. He has the right to choose his path. For now, he has to face his trials by the Shadows. And when he survives, he can choose where his life will take him."

"You Bitch, you are grooming him for ascension, aren't you?" Raven spit, as the words flew from her mouth.

"Daniel is capable of anything, but you will not be making any decisions for him. The Elders are watching every move that is made." Elizabeth was finished, and she turned to walk away.

Raven stood tall and opened her arms, spreading the black shrouded cape she wore. As she opened it fully, the material began to separate, and the forms of ravens flew from within the darkness. The swarm flew in two opposite directions, and met in the center flying circles around Elizabeth. As the ravens got closer and closer, they extended their claws and scratched at Elizabeth's exposed skin. She had been taken by surprise, but as she grew tired of the little game, she threw her hands out and an intense ethereal light engulfed the room.

As the light grew brighter, the ravens started to fall, one by one. They were not dead, but unconscious and powerless. Elizabeth laughed, as the opposing force became totally incapacitated. When the last bird was on the ground, Elizabeth turned and looked at them all scattered around in a circle. She knelt down and picked up one of the birds. "You stupid bottom feeder, did you think you could hurt me. If you can hear me, be warned. Daniel is, and always will, be property of the light."

Elizabeth turned and walked out the door of the barn, as she heard police sirens coming from down the road. She walked to an open place in the field and looked up. Satisfied with the end to the situation, she closed her eyes and a shaft of light formed around her.

Chapter Twenty: When Darkness Falls

Muerte turned to look at Malachi again. She tried to let go of her anger. She knew he was not to blame, but the idea of her death at his hands, was a lot to deal with. Then she looked back at the army she had led. Being under another's control, was something she was all too familiar with.

"Now that we have you back to being more of your former self. Please explain the army of the dead." Jen said, as she pointed to the zombie army that surrounded them.

"Just like Malachi, I was being controlled. Except in my case, I was a part of the dead. I was resurrected, to be of use in my abilities to claim the dead." She spoke.

"More of Abraxas' handywork." Daniel added.

"Yes, but how is this happening all around the world?" Elizabeth asked.

"It has all come from one source." Daniel said, as he pointed to Malachi. "He has the most of Abraxas' power. Just think of it, as a person with a split personality. Malachi did not know what was going on, and when Abraxas took over, he was in control. Somehow, he is doing his bidding at the same time as Malachi."

As he backed away from the group, Malachi started to cough. His face turned red, as if he were having convulsions. The others all looked on in disbelief, as he fell to the ground. Daniel began to move forward to go to his aid, but Muerte grabbed onto his arm and stopped him.

"No, stay back from this." Muerte insisted. "This is not a human thing. The demon is causing this. There is nothing we can do to save him now."

Daniel took a deep breath, because he did not want to just stand by and not do anything, while a person might possibly die. As Malachi tried to get back to his feet, he fell continually like a wounded animal. Then he fell forward and coughed hard, as he began to spit bile from his mouth.

The motion grew more and more erratic, before he finally spit a black oily substance out onto the ground. As he continued, the pool grew larger in size and looked like an oil spill. There seemed to be no stopping the flow, as Malachi heaved in pain.

Then as quickly as it began, it ended. Malachi fell backwards and gasped for air. He had turned blue from the inability to breathe. Looking down, he saw what had left his body, and he was scared. He wondered how this force had been inside him and taken control.

As Malachi stared deep into the dark pool, he could swear he saw movement. He looked hard, as he saw it again. There was something happening. He just did not know what. Then a part of the substance moved upwards into the air. First there was one peak, then another. In time there were five in all raising up, taking the form of fingers, soon to become a hand.

Malachi scooted backwards away from it, as an arm began to form. Muerte looked to Daniel, as if to say "now." Daniel flew forward, and as he ran, a blue streak formed behind him. He bounced out of sight, before stopping behind Malachi. With a quick grab, he took Malachi into the light and disappeared again, only to reappear next to Muerte.

"That my boy, was impressive. You had a great teacher." Muerte commented with a sly look on her face.

"Thanks." Elizabeth added.

Distracted by the rescue, no one was paying attention to the quickly forming body that came from the oil spill, except Jen.

"Guys, you need to see this." She called out, as she watched.

Turning, the group saw the hand had grown into a full body in just moments. They stood there, as the form, took an all too familiar shape. It was Abraxas, and he had formed a new body for himself.

"Hello little one. Did you miss me?" He said, as he made a gesture towards Jen.

Jen pulled back for a second, and then felt the rage in her body. "Didn't I already kill you?"

"Guess I am harder to get rid of, than you thought." He said as he began to laugh.

Chapter Twenty-One: Return Of The Demon

As Abraxas began to move, his appearance returned to normal, and his oily state disappeared. He stepped forward, and moved towards Jen. Backing up, she headed closer to Daniel. She felt unsure of what the demon had in mind.

"Ah, my legion of the dead, are here awaiting my return. Thank you Muerte, for making all this possible." He jabbed at her.

"I did nothing for you…willingly. I was one of the dead, and controlled. At least, I was…dead. Now I am more myself, and a little pissed off." She spoke, her voice filled with disgust.

"Be what you will, but this time, I am coming for what I want, and there will be no prisoners. So, choose your sides well." His arrogance filled his words, and the others grew worried at his intentions.

"Daniel, what can we do? We can't let this continue." Malachi sounded defeated.

"We will find a way to defeat him." Daniel tried to reassure him. "Malachi, you look different. What is happening?"

Muerte came to their side and looked at the boy. She raised his head and looked into his eyes. For a moment, she was speechless. Then, she lowered her hand, as she stroked his cheek. She was aware, and at the same time, concerned for him.

"He has been stripped of his darkness. Not just the part of Abraxas he had inside him. When Abraxas left, he took out the power I added, as an Angel of Death. There is no dark power here at all. Even what I instilled, is gone. The demon must have ripped it out when he left."

Malachi thought for a second about everything she said. Then he realized he was defenseless. His face grew white, as he began to understand the ramifications of his fate. Abraxas was more in control than ever.

"Daniel, what do I do now?" He asked. "I can't defend myself. I can't even help you. I am just human now."

Daniel looked at him, and observed the black veins that had covered his body, were now reverting to his true appearance. He looked like a different person, one which Daniel did not know. This new person, was vulnerable.

"You are not as defenseless as you think you are. You are still half angel, and I think you are about to get a crash course in what that means."

"We need to get to a safe place, so we can regroup and plan." Elizabeth commanded. "We cannot take him on like this. If Abraxas has all this power, we need to figure out what we are up against."

Before she could finish speaking, the dead began to move again. Abraxas stood safely out of the line of fire, as he commanded them to move in the direction of the group. The dead grew closer, and closed in, so no one could escape.

Each turned, so their backs were against each other. Elizabeth gave the cue to leave, as she saw the dead take ahold of Jen and Daniel. Elizabeth escaped with Muerte, but the others were trapped, as the dead clung to their arms, and did not allow their orbs to form.

"Funny isn't it, how the dead can dampen your powers, and even an orb, seems impossible. It's a pity you were just freed Malachi, just to be recaptured, to be a part of my army." The demon teased him.

"I don't think so. You see, my will power, is so much stronger than you believe. And I am not going down, just to satisfy you!" Malachi screamed out in anger, as he dove under the grasp of the dead.

Emerging outside the army, he ran for a memorial, where he grabbed a metal pole, that held up a flag for remembrance. As he charged back towards the army, he screamed, and as they turned to see him, he swung the pole, knocking them down one by one, until he cleared the way to Jen and Daniel.

"Ok, you are free, do something!" Malachi shouted.

"You got it." Jen yelled back, as she orbed over and took Malachi's hand.

They both disappeared into a bright light, as Daniel followed close behind. Abraxas stood watching, as they vanished. He smiled to himself, knowing he was the victor in this reunion.

From behind the mausoleum, a dark figure lurked, only coming forward, when the event was over. She walked up to Abraxas, and put her arms around him. He turned his face to her and smiled. "My dear Raven, you have done well. I feel stronger than ever. Those fools have no idea what is coming for them." As they both laughed, they were unaware another shadow loomed behind the stones.

Chapter Twenty-Two: Rise Of The Whitelighter

As her orb ended, Jen landed hard onto the stone surface, only gaining her balance as she grabbed for Malachi. He stumbled forward and caught himself from falling. Jen was not accustomed to taking visitors with her, but this time was necessary.

"Sorry about that, I had a little trouble compensating for your weight." Jen spoke, pressing her hands against her knees.

"It's Ok, you saved my life. I am sure Abraxas had plans for all of us." Malachi sounded relieved.

As they spoke, the others came forward. Elizabeth seemed relieved, they had made it safely to the stones, on top of the deserted mountain top. Jen looked around in amazement, at the state of the ruins. She smiled when she realized where they were.

"We are in Peru, does that mean this is…"

"The 15th-century Inca citadel Machu Picchu. It is one of my favorite getaway spots." Elizabeth said smiling. "This is where I taught Daniel to spread his wings and fly."

"Speaking of Daniel, where is he?" Muerte said, as she looked all around them.

"Wait, he was right behind us." Malachi added.

Just along the outer top wall of stone, a blue light formed. From within, Daniel flew forward, almost as if he was running. He tried to stop at the edge of the wall, only to overshoot the edge, and fly out into the open sky.

Daniel quickly remembered his training, as he extended his energy formed wings. As he plummeted to the ground, his wings extended and carried him upwards towards the highest wall. He landed just short of Jen, who looked on in amazement.

"How is it possible that you can do that? You never told me." She blasted him.

"I guess, even a boy has his secrets. I just never thought about sharing that one. Besides, after all we have been through, when did I have time?" He said, laughing at her.

"I am just relieved you are safe. What happened to delay you?" Elizabeth was curious.

"When I was leaving, I noticed there was someone else there besides Abraxas, so I took a detour to a darkened section of trees, and watched what was happening. It seems Raven was working with Abraxas all along. She came out of hiding, as soon as she thought we left."

"Raven saved him, when Jen thought she destroyed him. His power scattered, but she was there to collect it. Knowing all the time she could resurrect him eventually." Elizabeth added.

"And now he is more powerful than ever. How do we stop that?" Jen asked.

"By working together. As a group we are stronger. The last time you took him on, you were divided. Now there is more than just the three of you. You have an Angel of Death, and a new angel at your side." Muerte said, extending a hand towards Malachi.

"Yeah, but I am powerless. I have tried to focus the energy. Nothing comes, when I try to channel it."

"In time, it will. Just like with Daniel and Jen, it did not come easily or quickly. But it did happen. You just have to let go of the frustration and fear. You were born to this, and if someone had not tampered with you…you would have been further along." Elizabeth attempted to reassure him.

"Don't you feel anything inside, when you get excited or angry." Jen asked.

"No, nothing. When I had the dark energy, it was always there. I didn't have to think about it. I just feel empty inside."

"Maybe you just have to get really angry. It worked for me, when I woke up after my death, I was confused at first, then I wanted someone to pay. So, I channeled it, and took on a high-level demon." Jen said innocently. "Sometimes, you just have to be that pissed.

"Ok Lady Rambo. It is not all about needing or wanting to kill. It is more like having a need to do something. The power inside, will work to save you or another." Daniel added.

"Maybe you just need a jumpstart." Jen said, as she shoved Malachi off the wall behind him.

Malachi let out as scream, that echoed through the surrounding ruins. As he fell downward, Daniel looked down to him and prepared to fly. As Malachi tumbled through the air, he felt a change happening. It started as a tingling in his hands, that soon moved through his entire body.

He flipped, and saw the ground coming up fast, and he threw his hands outward and stopped, floating in mid-air. Daniel looked on in shock, before turning to Jen. He shook his head and swallowed the lump in his throat. He raised his hand to shake a finger at her, as to say no,

"What?" She asked. "He is safe, and I proved my point."

"Don't you ever pull a stunt like that again. Do you understand me?" Daniel was angry.

Below, Malachi floated above the stone structure, scared to move. He was not sure if he was angry or relieved, but he was sure of one thing. He felt the power within.

Chapter Twenty-Three: The War Of The Dead

Abraxas walked through the cemetery inspecting his army of the dead. He admired their obedience. His army of automatons was fearless, powerful and never stopped for injuries. He was sure they were more than a match for the living.

"Impressive, aren't they?' Raven spoke, as she came up from behind him.

"Yes, they will do well in the final battle. And they are rising worldwide." He added.

"Muerte was instrumental in calling the dead to rise. Now with the power you have inherited from Malachi, you can command them to your will."

"Excellent. I like how you said I inherited the power. So much nicer than stole, don't you think?" He laughed.

"So, what happens next?" Raven asked, sounding excited at the idea of world domination.

"It is simple, we eliminate this world, of the infestation of the living." Abraxas laughed, as he laid his black hat upon his head, and moved it into position. "Now, go forth and summon all the demons and other creatures, who would be willing to serve the new king of the underworld.

Raven lowered her head as to bow, before she shimmered from sight. She knew her task and set out to spread the word. She had secured her position in the new order. In the end, she had obtained power.

~~~~~~

Around the world, the dead continued to rise. Panic ensued for the living, who did not know how to deal with the situation. News reports filled the radio, internet, and television, of advancing populations of dead, who moved through the cities and occupied their spaces.
~~~~~~

Back on the mountain top, Elizabeth summoned all angels to her. They appeared quickly in groups and mass orbs. Joining the original group, they all became aware of the situation. War was coming, the balance of good and evil had tipped.

"How can we rid the world of dead. We help the innocent and defend against demons. This is entirely different." A voice called out.

"I hear you, and I understand your concerns. Muerte can instruct you on how to take down the dead, and put them back where they came from. It is not going to be easy. As with anything we tackle, we will make it happen together." Elizabeth turned away, as Muerte spoke.

As she instructed them, many were confused. They were asked to do something they had never before. Still, they knew what was upon them, and they prepared to go to all the corners of the earth for battle.

"I guess it is our turn." Malachi said trying to muster his courage.

"We'll be fine. We just have to manage the element of surprise." Daniel tried to comfort him. "We are going for Abraxas. Just remember, you have power and you know how to use it."

Malachi acknowledged him, as they all lifted to the sky, and one by one orbing to the cemetery where Abraxas stood with his army.

As they landed, the brightness of their light filled the area. Abraxas turned in shock, as they came in full strength upon him. For a moment, he questioned his army. Then he pulled upon his own power and began to take on the army of angels.

"Is this all you have?" He laughed. "The girl was better than this, the first time she scattered my energy.

"You might be surprised by how powerful we are." Jen jabbed at him.

"Then show it!" Abraxas screamed.

Just then, Malachi appeared in the sky above him. "Maybe this is what you are looking for."

Malachi threw his arms out as a bright light filled the sky, and his wings flapped back and forth. He smiled for a brief second, before unleashing his inner power. A feeling of confidence filled him, as he blasted Abraxas to the ground.

"I believe you stole something from me. Maybe, it is time you gave it back."

Malachi dropped down to Abraxas' side and placed his hand on the demon's head. As Malachi held on, a stream of black energy flowed back into him. Daniel saw what was happening, and turned to him in fear. This was not what they agreed to do.

After Malachi absorbed all his stollen energy, he lifted Abraxas off the ground and drug him upwards. As they climbed, Abraxas hung there defenseless. Malachi had won, but for what goal.

The power surged through Malachi, as he began to change. The darkness, merged with his pure white angel light, morphing and turning into something unnatural. As the new power surged through his body, Malachi tossed Abraxas to the ground breaking him.

Daniel came to his side, to see the broken remains of the demon, and witness Malachi landing along-side. As he turned to Daniel, his eyes began to change again. Now, they looked like a glowing demonic dark fire.

"What did you do?" Daniel said, looking on, as Malachi's body continued to change.

"I took what was mine, and now, I am the one with all the power. And the rest of you are nothing…correction…less than nothing."

Malachi took to the air again, this time using his power to reactivate the dead, and then turn his power on the angels who were once on his side.

"Maybe today, is a good day to die!" he screamed

Included next are the first chapters of G.W. Mullins' Best-Selling title

**From The Dead Of Night Book One –
Daniel Is Waiting**

From
The
Dead
Of
Night
Book Series

Death is only the beginning.
Daniel walked in the land of the Dead.
Now the Dead want him back

Daniel Is Waiting

Daniel Returns

Daniel Awakens

G.W. Mullins

Daniel's Fate

From The Dead Of Night Book One
Extended Anniversary Edition
Death is only the beginning
Daniel Is Waiting
A Ghost Story
G.W. Mullins

From The Dead Of Night Book One –
Daniel Is Waiting

Is Available in Hardback (978-1-64516-874-4),
Paperback (978-1-64516-873-7) and various eBook
formats worldwide.

ghost

gōst/

noun

noun: ghost; plural noun: ghosts

1.   an apparition of a dead person that is believed to appear or become manifest to the living, typically as a nebulous image.

"the building is haunted by the ghost of a nun"

synonyms: specter, phantom, wraith, spirit, presence

Sixty Years Ago

"Mom why are you being so crazy about this? I just want to know the truth." Daniel pleaded with Emily, but she became more outraged. The final threads of the lie she and her husband had hidden for sixteen years was unraveling. Daniel had stumbled onto the truth. Being a head strong teenager meant he was not going to give up easily and let it rest.

"Daniel, sometimes the past is better left in the past. Why won't you just leave this all alone before you cause more problems than ever imagined." Emily pleaded with him.

"No, I want the truth. Is the woman I saw with dad, my mother, or are you. I am tired of being lied to. I have felt my whole life something was wrong. I don't know how but I have always known, didn't you see how as a child I would never call you Mommy? Damn-it, tell me the truth."

"Ok, you want the truth, then I will give it to you. You are not my son. You are the bastard child of my husband and his secretary. While I was home being the loving and devoted wife, your dad was out screwing around. He thought he wouldn't get caught. Well guess what, when you get another woman pregnant, then you get caught. At least my children will be born into a house of marriage." Emily spewed forth all the hatred she had pushed down for so long.

She reveled in delight as she unloaded years of pain and hatred. She never thought about the fact it was aimed at the wrong person. Emily's husband should have been her target, instead of an innocent sixteen-year-old boy, who bore the load of his father's sin.

Daniel stared on in disbelief as he tried to conceive how such a thing could be true. The man he had loved and respected his whole life had been living a lie. And what was worse, he had made

Daniel live that lie as well. His whole world began to crash around him. Nothing and no one he ever believed in was real anymore. They were just a group of actors, each one playing the roles they assigned themselves.

A tear ran down Daniel's face as he looked into Emily's eyes. She was as much a victim as he was. Confusion filled his mind as he searched for any clear way to accept any of it. All he knew was that he wanted to get out of the house of lies that was closing in around him. He turned and headed for the door as a look of terror crept across Emily's face. Her only thought was. 'What have I done?'

Daniel raced for the door before Emily could plead with him not to go. She knew what she had done was wrong. She knew when James came home from work, there would be hell to pay for this. She had to fix the mess she had made. She had to keep Daniel at home and persuade him not to tell his father what he found out.

Emily raced for the door and grabbed her keys. Daniel had to be nearby, there wasn't enough time for him to get far. As she raised the garage door, the rain poured on her head. She worked quickly to get down the drive, but in her confusion, she backed the car into the side porch before squealing tires and heading for the main road.

As she drove, the rain pelted her windshield. The old wipers were too shredded to keep the window clear. Emily could barely see as the tears burned her eyes and the windshield started to fog over. Rounding the corner, she didn't see Daniel walking by the road. As she tried to wipe the windshield, the car swerved towards the edge.

Daniel heard the sound of the car coming at him, but it was too late to move. He looked into the headlight's bright white glow as the car ran him down. As he fell to the ground unconscious, his last thoughts were almost humorous. He started life as an accident and now he would die that same way.

Emily jumped from the car and frantically ran to his side. Time stopped for her in that moment. Everything around her froze as she felt the pain hit her heart so hard it was as if it was going to explode. She screamed out for help, hoping someone, anyone would hear her. She just sat there in her frozen state cradling Daniel in her arms. She only whispered in Daniel's ear, "I am so sorry…I was wrong."

~~~~~~

Daniel was rushed to the hospital in a comatose state. Days and weeks went by but there was no change in his condition. Visitors came and went, but one regular guest was always present…Janet Blakely. She had allowed Daniel's father to take him from her at birth, she wasn't going to allow the same thing in death. She cared for Daniel just as if he was a small child. She read to him, told him stories about her life and shared her dreams of what he would become. In the matter of a
~~~~~~

few short weeks, she shared a lifetime with him. And in the end, she shared his death.

Daniel died peacefully. His mother sitting beside him stroking his short dark blond hair. A lump rose up in her throat as she realized he wasn't breathing. Janet called for the doctors, but there was nothing they could do. They only told her, he had gone to a better place. She looked at the doctors in a blind rage wondering how anyone would think of death as being a better alternative to life.

Janet walked to Daniel's bed as the doctors and nurses left. Taking his hand, she said her goodbyes as her heart filled with regret. Maybe if she had not given him up, he would still be alive. As she released his hand, she removed the ring he was wearing. It was a class ring with a brilliant blue stone. She held it close to her heart and cried, as the nurse came to escort her out.

When Janet got home, she placed the ring in her jewelry box. She had to put her secret to rest. If her husband found out, she knew he would leave. A hidden part of her life was over. Her last act before she closed the jewelry box, was to phone the local paper and place an obituary for her son Daniel Blakely. As the call ended, the lid of the jewelry box closed and its rhythmic music ended.

~~~~~~

At the funeral home the next day James and Emily viewed the body of their son for the last time. James had not let go of his anger, it had only mixed with his grief and made him intolerable at times. As James looked at the remains of his son, he noticed the school ring was missing from Daniel's hand. He flew into a rage questioning the director of the funeral home, but he was told there never had been a ring and it probably didn't make it from the hospital.

As they approved the casket and the body, the lid was closed. Daniel's body was laid to rest the next day. It should have been an ending to a very unfortunate destructive situation. It was not. Death
~~~~~~

is an unexplainable mystery. We think of life and death by human terms. But the dead have another existence all their own. Sometimes, death is only the beginning.

As the crowds died down and the mourners left the graveside, there was a stillness in the air. The family car pulled away passing Janet as she watched from a distance. The casket was placed into the mausoleum, as a breeze swept across the cemetery grounds. It swirled and kicked up leaves and debris. In the center of the whirlwind formed a blue light. The light grew brighter and larger unseen to anyone in the area that was living. The dead however, watched intently to see what was happening. As the light formed a long shaft, a form emerged taking the shape of a young blond-haired man.

The light dissipated as Daniel opened his eyes and reached his hand to his head. The feeling was like he had a head ache. He was groggy and hung over. He looked around at the tombstones and shook his head wondering how he had gotten there. He was

confused but who wouldn't be when waking up
dead?

Today

"I'm worried about you Jen. What will you do when I am gone? "She hadn't thought much about it.

"You can't stay here by yourself. It's not safe. I mean, when there were more of us kids at home, then we could help each other when they would fight. You don't stand a chance by yourself."

"Aww Jay.... you know me, I can always find a place to hide."

"Like where?"

"Maybe the attic" Jen laughed. She knew Jay was aware she was terrified of the attic and the possibility of mice.

"You have to think this out before I go. It's not safe with mom and dad's fighting and it's not safe on the streets with the gangs roaming the area."

Jen knew she was in a bad situation and there was no time for joking. She also knew if she didn't convince Jay she would be OK, that he wouldn't leave for school. He had worked too hard to get in there, and she couldn't ruin it for him.

"I can always stay with friends," Jen said unconvincingly. She knew this wasn't a solution, she had just a couple of good friends and their parents would get suspicious if she was there too much. Deep inside she wished she was going off to school too. Away from her parent's constant arguing and the violence that often followed.

Jen thought about her parents and how with all the other kids gone, everything would fall on her. Her mom had depended on Jay for everything, and with him gone and her dad being the abuser he was, the future didn't look too bright. She had to take care of herself. 'It was clear no one else was going to,' she thought to herself and wondered why people had kids if they didn't want to take care of them. The thought of being unwanted almost made her cry but she had to stay strong and keep a brave face for Jay. She couldn't let him know how lost she felt.

She took a deep breath and looked up across the street. In front of them was a huge cemetery, with acres of graves and mausoleums and a huge caretaker's house. She hadn't been inside for a long time, and her memory of it was vague. The place was surrounded by a huge iron fence with black metal bars that were charged with electricity. The only way in and out was through a main gate and it was monitored by a guard. 'The local gangs couldn't get in,' she thought to herself. 'It's the cemetery or nothing'.

Oddly, Jen wasn't scared of the cemetery. It just seemed peaceful and quiet. In her mind she almost felt drawn to it. She wondered what it would be like to hide out there. She would only be there when her parents fought. Trouble was, that was most of time when they were home. She studied the fence line and all the way down the street, until she saw it, a little wooden gate. It was probably locked, but there was enough room for her to slide in under it. She was thin and never had a problem squeezing into small spaces.

"Umm Jay...what about the cemetery?" Jen blurted out.

"Are you crazy? You can't get in there and even if you could, why would you want to? That place creeps me out."

"I think I can get in. There is a gate, and it has a small opening underneath and I think I could fit through."

"Someone would see you."

"Who? Nobody lives near the gate. It's near the abandoned houses. And I am sure no one lives in the house inside the cemetery. It's probably a caretaker's house that no one uses anymore."

"You can't be sure of that," Jay looked at her as if she was crazy.

"I think this will work and no one will see me at night. No one lives over there and if I slip in quickly enough, I will be fine."

Jay just looked at her in disbelief, "Do you really think you can pull this off?"

"Jay...I can do this. I have to do this. You can't just not go to school after all you went through to get in, and I don't see any other choice," Jen pleaded with him.

"Ok, you've convinced me. It's gotta be safer in there than out here at home."

"Now we just have to test my theory."

They waited until dark, and then Jen went about proving her point. She easily slipped through the gate and was inside with no one the wiser. Jay felt calmer, and at the same time creeped out. He had just agreed to leave his fifteen-year-old sister alone with his violent parents and her only outlet was a cemetery full of dead people. 'What could go wrong?' He thought sarcastically to himself. Jen looked around and decided that there was plenty of cover inside for her to hide from anyone who was looking for her. She just wasn't sure what to do if she had to spend the night.

As she turned to leave, she heard a sound. As quiet as a whisper, it sounded a lot like someone saying "Hello". She turned quickly thinking she had been caught. Fear rushed over her and she felt her face turning red. But as she spun around on her heels, she saw no one. There was only Jay guarding the gate she had come through. Jen convinced herself it was nerves and she had invented the whole thing in her head. She headed back to the gate and let herself out as easily as she came in.

As they walked away from the cemetery, Jen looked up to see a couple of the guys from the local gang heading in their direction. She grabbed Jay by the arm and drug him towards their yard. As the guys passed, they gave Jay a look. They knew he had gotten into a school and would be out of their reach soon. They weren't really happy about losing out on a new dealer.

"So, what do you do if you have to stay all night?" Jay asked.

"I don't know, I could go to the old house but only after I watch for a while to see that no one lives there. Maybe I will just go into one of the mausoleums if they are open." She laughed at the thought.

"If the weather was bad, that is not the worst idea. They probably do not lock them." Jay said shaking as if the idea scared him.

"Oh Jay, you're such a girl. Just picture the idea of sleeping in a room with dead people."

"Well, they are in coffins inside the walls you know. It's not like you will be propped up with your feet on one doing your homework." He laughed.

"Yeah, you've got a point. And it beats getting a broken arm or worse at home."

She remembered when Jay had gotten in the way one time when her dad had thrown a chair at their mother. It ended in a trip to the emergency room and a huge doctor bill that led to another fight when they got home. She didn't like the idea of ending up the same way. She didn't want to admit it to Jay, but she was a little scared. But if she had to do it, she would. She couldn't get in the way of his future.

"I feel a little better about the situation but I will still worry about you. Be careful of mom and dad, and watch out for the gangs. And please don't ever let anyone know you are in the house alone. Promise me!"

"I promise, I'll be careful and I will write to you as much as possible."

As Jen turned back to look at the cemetery, she felt a weird feeling overtake her. Almost as if she was being welcomed there. She studied the fence line, while sitting on the porch with Jay. As she looked at the gate, she was sure there was someone inside looking back at her. He was a blond-haired boy about her age she thought. She blinked in disbelief and when she focused again, he was gone. She shook her head, and decided she had to be mistaken. No one could be gone that quickly. It all had to be in her imagination.

"Just promise me you will be OK," Jay said smiling at her.

She turned to him and made a goofy face, "You know I was always the smartest of us all."

"Yeah, I guess you are right, but I'm still your older brother and it's my prerogative to worry."

"Well don't! What's the worst that could happen? I could run into a ghost or something?"

They both laughed not wanting to let on to the other how scared they really were.

Chapter 1: The Escape

It didn't take a day's time before the fighting started up again. Jen's parents were louder than she had ever heard them and just as violent. She just couldn't understand how they could fight so much and stay together. She did know, she had to get out. Trouble was, getting out meant going through the room that had been designated ground zero. But even if she did get out, where would she go, it was 11 P.M.? It wasn't like she could just go to the library or a friend's house.

She quietly crept from her room and down the hall towards the living room. Ever so quietly, she tried to move without being heard or even worse seen. She peeked into the doorway just as a picture frame came crashing into the opening. Jen jerked back in fear. That was too close. She was able to jump past the opening of the doorway while her parents had their backs to her. In a few seconds, she was in the kitchen with her hand on the back-door knob.

Jen turned the knob and pulled the door gently towards her. She quietly prayed to herself that the hinges would not squeak. As soon as she had the door open just enough for her to slip through, she was out the door. She made her way into the yard before falling to her knees. The exhilaration and fear had her heart pounding in her chest. She knew, fear or not, she had to keep her head together and get to safety.

Jen didn't understand why her parents had to fight. She had been over it again and again in her head and it just didn't make sense. Her older sister Carrie said it was because they were just unhappy people. That didn't make sense to Jen. Just because you are unhappy, doesn't give you a reason to hurt other people and not act like a parent. None of her other friends had this problem, and sometimes, she wished she lived in one of their houses and could have a normal life.

She remembered the times when all the kids were still at home. When there were five of them, it was easier to stick together. But after her older brother Tim went to a correctional facility for getting mixed up with drugs and the local gang, and Carrie got a job away from the area, then there were only herself, Jay and little Johnny.

She tried not to think about Johnny. His was probably the cruelest fate of them all. She remembered the night when their parents started to break furniture and all the kids hid in the dining room. Johnny was too young to understand the fighting. He tore loose of Carrie's arms and ran from the house and into the road. Unfortunately, the car he ran in front of just couldn't stop in time. Jen thought that this might have been the point where her parents stopped caring about the kids all together.

The past year without the others was ok because Jen and Jay could hide easily together. But now Jay had gone to school and she was alone. For the first time there was no one there to protect her, and she knew what might happen.

She had no choice. If she was going to survive, it wasn't going to be at home. She had to go into the cemetery. When she and Jay went there originally, it didn't seem like such a bad idea. But now, facing the darkness of the place from the sidewalk just in front, she wasn't so sure. Her fears were overtaking her and she felt her hands start to shake. Could she really pull this off? She had to control her fear. There was no other choice. She had to do this one alone.

As she walked, Jen thought about how things were lately at home. Her dad had been away a lot with work and that seemed to make her mother happy. He worked construction and would be gone for a week at a time. Trouble was, he would come home and usually he would be tired and mean. Maybe work wasn't the only reason he stayed away.

Maybe he just didn't want to come home or he had another place to go. Whatever he was doing, the family did not know for sure.

When he was home, he stayed to himself as much as possible. The kids didn't really approach him for fear of his temper. Everyone knew that when he was angry, it was better to be invisible. Jen's mother tried to be invisible at first but it didn't last for long. Especially if she had to ask him for money to pay the bills. A lot of their fights started with money and dealing with being a family.

Jen's mom worked as much as she could, and made a bit of money as a waitress in a bar, but it wasn't enough to pay the bills. That was what the latest fight was about, her mom in the bar around other men. Her dad wanted the money to come in but not if it meant his wife was around men.

Funny thing was, as much as Jen's dad wanted her mom to work and make money, he also wanted her home to do all the cleaning and do things around the house. No matter what they were doing, Jen felt invisible to them. She was sure of one thing; they weren't paying much attention to her. She barely remembered the last time her father spoke to her. It was a similar situation with her mother as well.

So, this is what it had all come to…standing on a street corner outside of a cemetery. Jen felt a chill shoot down her spine.   The feeling was odd; she was feeling part fear, part exhilaration. She hadn't felt anything like it before, but at the same time she was excited. This felt like an adventure. It was a chance to get away from her life and craziness for just a little while. It was an escape.

She walked quickly to the little gate and paid close attention to her surroundings. If she was seen, this would be a one-time trip. Luckily, it was late at night and the tree lined streets were very dark. She scanned down the sidewalk and looked for anyone that might be able to see her. There was no one. As soon as she was sure it was safe, she slipped under the gate and was inside the cemetery wall.

In a few seconds, she found a hiding place inside a hedge of bushes. The growth was so thick, she was sure no one would see her. Her heart was racing in her chest and she could feel it thumping. She did it! She was proud of herself. She thought to herself, 'If she had to hide in a cemetery, this wasn't so bad.' Jen leaned back against a tree, folded her arms around her knees and took a deep breath and sighed in relief. She quietly giggled to herself and was so proud of what she had accomplished.

She had never thought about what it would be like to be inside a cemetery at night. The closest she got was that day before Jay left. It wasn't nearly as bad as she would have imagined. What was there to be afraid of? Everyone was dead. She was warm enough sitting in her pile of leaves in the hedge. The fall weather had not turned too cold.

As she calmed herself, and her heart rate went back to normal, she scanned the cemetery. Had anyone lived in the old house on the grounds? Jay said it was a caretaker's house but did anyone use it anymore? She decided not. If someone lived there, then there would be lights on or people moving around. These were things she never saw when she looked at the house. She stared at the house and studied its features as much as she could in the dark. It looked abandoned and lonely. Kind of like her.

As she looked at the house, she realized it had no curtains downstairs. If someone lived there, the windows would be covered in blinds or something. The house had older features like the ones from old pictures. The front porch had detailed carvings around the top of the roof. They were pretty but people didn't do that anymore. And the walls were covered in paint that was peeling after years of exposure. She decided it was a house like her grandma would have once lived in.

For a moment, Jen thought about a happier time when her grandma was still alive. Things were different then; she hadn't realized it until now. Her grandma's house was nice and filled with nice things. The more she thought about it, the bigger the lump in her throat became. She never really spoke of grandma and didn't really think about her that much.

A flood of memories came back, about her childhood and how the family lived with grandma that time her dad had left for a long time. Her mom had to work a lot to pay the bills and was not around much. Grandma took care of them all. It wasn't easy on her since she was ill a lot, but she loved the kids so much. She would tell them stories and make them her special cookies. Jen thought there was nothing better than grandma's cookies and one of her stories. She wouldn't have minded some of those cookies and a story now. She was getting hungry and the comfort of a story would have done wonders for her. A fantasy story had to be better than where was now.

Thinking of grandma brought a smile to her face, but it also made her think about her brothers and sister. Where were they and what were they doing? She laughed to herself, when she felt sure they weren't hiding in a cemetery in the middle of the night. A shiver ran down her spine again. She was kind of cold when the wind blew, but the feeling was almost as if she was being watched. The thought made her more than a bit paranoid.

Jen glanced around and saw no one, but she still felt the feeling as if someone was there. She became restless and thought that she might need to explore a bit to see what might be a round. She knew it would not be a good idea to go home until morning. The lights were still on at her house and she could see her mom and dad still moving around. Besides, she didn't want to creep back in, just to wind up in the middle of their fight.

Jen decided she needed a place out of the direct path the wind. The temperature wasn't that bad, but the grass under the leaves was a bit damp. She didn't want to chance the house. Even if no one lived there, there might be a watchman who checked the grounds at night. Perhaps the mausoleum, which was just a few yards away. If she made a break for it, the hedges would protect her from being seen.

As she tried to work up the nerve to move, there was a weird noise in the distance. Jen couldn't quite make it out but it sounded mechanical. As she focused on the sound, it got closer and closer. The sound was like a mechanical engine. She tried to determine what direction it was coming from. As the sound got louder, she looked around the cemetery road ways and saw a light headed right for her. She thought to herself that maybe hiding in a cemetery was not a good idea after all.

The sound was louder now and the light shined in her direction. Her heart sank in her chest, she was sure she was caught, by whoever or whatever it was.

Chapter 2: At Night in The Cemetery

Jen didn't know what to do. If she ran, she would be seen and if she stayed, she most certainly would be found. She decided the best thing to do was stay curled up behind the bushes and see what happened. The noise was right behind her and the light lit up the whole area where she was hiding. She looked through the bushes and saw what was coming, and to her amazement, her fear faded immediately. It was a short fat man on a motor scooter. She almost laughed at how comical the man looked. In her mind, he kind of looked like a circus clown. At once she realized he was not coming for her, but making rounds on the road behind her.

The little scooter turned the corner beside her and moved away. As soon as he was out of sight, she laughed. How could she have panicked so much over a fat guy on a scooter? And then she thought, maybe this was what she needed, to convince herself that she was safe. Her fear was gone now and a weird sense of calm filled her. But what was she to do now?

She was sure there would not be any more security runs for a while. Why would they need to continuously check the grounds? But if she was going to be coming here often, she would have to figure out the guard's schedule. But for now, it was almost 1 A.M., and it was getting colder. She decided that shelter was necessary, and the house might be too dangerous. Even though the guard did not check the house, it still seemed too risky. Her only other option was the big mausoleum.

Jen jumped to her feet and worked her way around the hedges as fast as possible making her way to the door. As she reached out for it, her heart began to beat loudly again. She quietly chanted to herself, "Please be unlocked, please be unlocked, please be unlocked." And to her surprise, it was, she moved inside quickly, hoping she wasn't seen by anyone.

As she made her way in, the inside of the room was very dark. Her eyes were used to the darkness outside, but it was even darker in the mausoleum. She closed the door behind her and stepped in as far as she dared without knowing where she was going. Within a minute or two, her eyes adjusted to the room. There were only two windows and both of them were covered with multicolored stained glass. The light coming through them was very little and did not illuminate the room well enough to see.

She moved towards the bigger of the windows and could see the shapes in the glass with the help of a local street light. It was a beautiful scene that looked like something from the bible. Since her family wasn't very religious, she couldn't place the image, but it looked like something her grandmother had shown her as a child when she would read stories to the children. The familiarity was comforting for a moment. The rest of the place however, was not so much. She could now see the place more clearly. Everything looked like stone or marble and it all reminded her of a cold smelly basement.

She moved from wall to wall trying to make out as much as she could. The place seemed to be clean. But then again, why would it be dirty? It's not like people would be coming and going through there like a normal house. Jen giggled and said to herself, "It's actually cleaner than home." She thought this must be true because her mother didn't really try to keep the place up and had often put the housecleaning off on the kids. But as they got older and left one by one, the amount of maid's service was pretty much all gone. All that was left was Jen now, and with school and the fights, it was near impossible for her to do much.

Jen walked around close to the walls and ran her fingers over the small squares that were in several places. Each had been engraved with about a sentence or two on it. It was hard to read, but what she could not make out with her eyes, she could sometimes feel with her finger tips. It seemed a lot of these people interned here were from decades ago and a few from as much as a hundred years before. She found it fascinating that people from a single family had continued to bring their relatives here. Jen thought long and hard about how close this family must have been, and how she barely remembered where her grandmother was buried. She hadn't visited her once over all these years. She decided if she could see her way through all this, that would be one thing she would correct.

While walking around Jen's eyes had adjusted as well as they could to the low light and she found the place to be more inviting than earlier. After all, she thought, who in the mausoleum was going to object to her being here or bother her. She had seen a bench on one wall. She had earlier kicked it accidentally and she decided this was as good a place as any to relax and settle in for the night.

As she leaned back, she felt something odd behind her head. It felt like something sticking out of the wall. She ran her hand over it and realized that one of the marker stones had a picture attached to it. She ran her fingers across it to try and clear the little dust that had collected. She could barely make out the image in the dark, bit appeared to be a very good-looking boy, probably a teenager, but she was not sure. His name however she was sure of ... Daniel. He had died in the 1960's. How sad she thought, that he could have died so young. She thought of her brother and how many other people were here in the cemetery that barely lived before they were gone. The thought made her sad.

She wondered what Daniel's life might have been like. She had always loved TV and movies and thought he might have been like James Dean or something back in the time when guys wore leather jackets and drove classic cars. She liked this version of him and decided she would hold on to it. It was comforting to think about Daniel. He was taking her mind off of everything else. It didn't do much for the chill in the air though. It was nice to be inside, but all the stone was adding to the coldness of the place. She was just happy to be dry and out of the wind though.

Jen decided if she was to come back here again, then next time she would bring a backpack with a few things. A flash light was a must, and something to eat and some water. She would need a sweater or something to wrap up in. She wished she had all these things right now, but there was nothing she could do about it. She just curled up into a ball on the bench and laid her head back onto Daniel's stone. Jen had never thought about the idea of having a boyfriend, but Daniel, she thought, might be a lot like what she would have wanted. Well, if he was alive and in her time. Sad thing was…he wasn't.

Jen's eyes grew heavy and she steadily drifted off to sleep. She knew she was in for the night and creeping back home would be a mistake. Besides what if the fight was still going on? She put the whole thing out of her head, yawned and was out. As she dreamed, her mind was filled with images of

Daniel. She didn't even know him and she dreamed of him like she had known him her whole life. Her life was different in the dreams, there was no fighting, she was safe and he was there to protect her. The dream made her happy. She felt like she needed protecting, now more than ever.

At around 3 A.M., she jerked awake. She heard a noise but didn't quite know what it was. She was very groggy and out of it. It took a few minutes to focus. The sound happened once, then again. She thought to herself, 'Could it have been the security guard again?' Had she slept through one of his rounds? She wasn't sure. Then it happened again, it was a funny sound, but not the scooter. It almost sounded as if it was in the room with her. She panicked and thought to herself, 'Oh no, is someone here with me?'

She sat up and scanned the room but saw no movement. It didn't make sense, but the sounds were coming every few minutes and were getting a little louder. She stood up and walked around the room trying to make sense of what was going on. As she moved about, the sound got quieter like she had moved further away from it. The noise was really only loud when she was near Daniel. She thought maybe that is why it was loud enough to wake her from her sleep. Jen had rested her head near the source of the noise. It wasn't really loud at all, just coming from the wall.

Jen whispered out loud, "Hello". It was almost as if she was expecting a response. But none came. Just the occasional popping noise. The noise sounded electrical, but why would a cemetery put electricity into a place like this? It wouldn't make sense. "The dead have no need for lights," she thought to herself. And just as soon as she finished her sentence, the popping noise happened several times in a row.

The sound didn't scare Jen as much as it puzzled her. She wanted to know what it was and if she was safe, but at the same time she did not feel like she was in danger. She sat back down and turned to Daniel and said, "If you were here, you would protect me. Wouldn't you?" She knew it was silly to speak to him as if here were there, but since there was no one to answer her, she didn't care. Just as soon as she was done with her question, a series of pops happened again. Almost as if it were an answer to what she said.

Jen didn't know what to make of it all. She did realize how tired she was and she really needed more sleep. She curled back up like before and drifted off to sleep again. As she slept, her hands were tucked under her head and in between herself and the stone with Daniel's name on it. Her last thought as she was fading out, was how much she wished she could talk to Daniel. And then she was asleep again.

During the night she slept through the rounds the guard made and even the popping noises that were now even louder than before. The sounds had begun to take a new form now, almost like a version of Morse Code. It was probably just as well that Jen could not hear them, or know that she was not alone anymore.

About the Author

Thanks for choosing this book, if you enjoyed it, please leave positive feedback.

G.W. Mullins is an Author, Photographer, and Entrepreneur of Native American / Cherokee descent. He has been a published author for over 13 years. His writing has focused on the paranormal and Native American studies.

Mullins has released several books on the history/stories/fables of the Native American Indians. Among his books are the extremely successful "Star People, Sky Gods and Other Tales of the Native American Indians," "Story Teller An Anthology Of Folklore From The Native American Indians," "The Native American Story Book - Stories Of The American Indians For Children Volumes 1-5," "The Native American Cookbook," and "Walking With Spirits Native American Myths, Legends, And Folklore Volumes 1 Thru 6."

He has released the complete series of his Sci/fi Fantasy books "From The Dead Of Night," including the Best-Selling titles – "Daniel Is Waiting" and "Daniel Returns." His most recent work includes the series "Rise Of The Snow Queen" featuring Book One "The Polar Bear King", Book Two "War Of The

Witches", and Book Three "The Story of Gerda And Kai."

Mullins' latest releases include two young adult fantasy series, "Rise of the Darklighter" Book One "Dark Awakening" and the "Dream Walker" Book Series featuring "Enter the Sandman" and "Wide Awake In Dream Land."

Among his other releases are "The Legend Of White Bear" (a Native American paranormal shapeshifting story), "Messages from The Other Side" (a nonfiction book about communication with the dead), and the currently releasing "The Convergence" (a post-apocalyptic book multi-series event)

For further information, on his writing, visit G.W. Mullins' web site at ***http://gwmullins.wix.com/books***.

What begins as a simple, bittersweet tale about a man turned into a polar bear, grandly unfolds into a rich, mythical adventure, in this best-selling book series.

Based on Hans Christian Andersen's fairy tale, author G.W. Mullins expands on this classic story creating a new mythology that takes readers into the land of snow and ice.

G.W. Mullins

Rise Of The Snow Queen
Book Series

The Polar Bear King
War Of The Witches
The Story of Gerda and Kai

<u>Also Available From G.W. Mullins</u>

The Convergence Book One Mass Destruction

The Convergence Book Two Armageddon

The Lend Of White Bear (Extended Edition)

Rise Of The Snow Queen Book One The Polar Bear King

Rise Of The Snow Queen Book Two The War Of The Witches

Rise Of The Snow Queen Book Three The Story Of Gerda And Kai

Daniel Awakens A Ghost Story Begins– From The Dead Of Night Prequel

Daniel Is Waiting A Ghost Story – From The Dead Of Night Book One

Daniel Returns A Ghost Story - From The Dead Of Night Book Two

Night of The Demon

Daniel's Fate A Ghost Story Ends - From The Dead Of Night Book Four

Dream Walker Book One Enter The Sand Man

Dream Walker Book Two Wide Awake In Dream Land

Nick Grainger Book One The Curse Of Cleopatra

Nick Grainger And The Return Of Anubis Book Two

The Legend Of White Bear

Messages From The Other Side Stories of the Dead, Their Communication, and Unfinished Business

Vengeance

Mysteries Of The Unseen World – Ghost, Hauntings and The Unexplained

Haunted America Stories Of Ghost, Hauntings And The Unexplained

Timeless – A Paranormal Romance Murder Mystery

Mullins

Star People, Sky Gods, And Other Tales Of The
Native American Indians

More Star People, Sky Gods, And Other Paranormal
Tales Of The Native American Indians

Lost Tales Of The Native American Indians Vol 1

Walking With Spirits Native American Myths,
Legends, And Folklore Volumes One Thru Six

The Native American Cookbook

Native American Cooking - An Indian Cookbook
With Legends And Folklore

The Native American Story Book - Stories Of The
American Indians For Children
Volumes One Thru Five

The Best Native American Stories For Children

Cherokee A Collection of American Indian Legends,
Stories And Fables

Creation Myths - Tales Of The Native American
Indians

Night of The Demon

Strange Tales Of The Native American Indians

Spirit Quest - Stories Of The Native American
Indians

Animal Tales Of The Native American Indians

Medicine Man - Shamanism, Natural Healing,
Remedies And Stories Of The Native American
Indians

Native American Legends: Stories Of The Hopi
Indians Volumes One and Two

Totem Animals Of The Native Americans

The Best Native American Myths, Legends And
Folklore Volumes One Thru Three

Ghosts, Spirits And The Afterlife In Native American
Indian Mythology And Folklore

War Song: Tales Of The Native American Indians

Origin Tales Of The Native American

As the city darkens and humans descend into sleep, a powerful entity known as the Sand Man, takes control of our dreams and nightmares.
DREAM WALKER
Don't Fall Asleep, The SandMan is Coming!
Enter The SandMan
Wide Awake In Dreamland
Available in Hardback, Paperback and eBook
G.W. Mullins

For books available from G.W. Mullins in Hardback, Paperback and eBook

Visit: https://gwmullins.wixsite.com/books

Or scan the QR Code below

Links to G.W. Mullins pages are on Linktree
https://linktr.ee/gw.mullins

9 781958 221198